W9-AZH-921

Nia & the numbers game

A Teenager's Guide to Education, Relationships & Sex

Kela Henry, MD

Published by BTH Creations LLC

ISBN: 978-0-9995-7360-0 (sc)
ISBN: 978-0-9995-7363-1 (hc)
ISBN: 978-0-9995-7361-7 (e)

Library of Congress Control Number: 2018901291

Lulu Publishing Services rev. date: 05/10/2018

Contents

Foreword

Growing up, I always knew I was going to college. I just knew. I wasn't sure exactly what I wanted to be when I grew up, but, as cliché as it sounds, I knew that I wanted to help people. My parents were serious about education and made it clear what they expected of my sister Anetra and me. Mom and Dad did not have the same opportunities to attend college right after high school, so they worked hard and sacrificed to make sure that my sister and I did.

Without having actually been through the college experience themselves, my parents' advice was just to keep my grades up and to "be a good girl." However, there is much more to higher education than just academics. My book focuses on the emotional and social aspects of high school and college experiences as they pertain to African-American and Hispanic girls.

I have been a guest speaker at various nonprofit engagements in the Atlanta area for the past few years. In this role, I learned how important it is to educate teenage girls about preparing for the future physically, emotionally and academically. I knew I wanted to write a book about these topics. Initially it was a challenge for me to convey what I wanted in writing so that it would resonate with young readers. I decided that instead of using my own voice throughout, I would create a relatable character. The first name that came to mind for the heroine in this character-driven story was Nia, from a word in Swahili, an East African language, meaning purpose. Nia's purpose is *edutainment*, combining education and entertainment so that my readers will learn while enjoying Nia's story. The book title struck me like lightning as I was commuting home from work one day. "NIA & THE NUMBERS GAME!" I thought. "I like the alliteration of it and the way it rolls off the tongue." The book takes on this theme as each chapter title includes a reference to a relevant number. For example, 1881 is the year Spelman College was founded and is the title of Chapter Seven when Nia starts her freshman year on campus.

The book follows Nia from middle school through medical school, which includes those years when young ladies' bodies and attitudes are changing and decisions are made (or not made) that affect their futures forever. I hope that NIA & THE NUMBERS GAME provides the insights to readers that I was looking for when making the transition into young adulthood. Nia and her supporting cast are loveable and relatable characters, and I'm in there also at the end of every chapter having a conversation with the reader. I want the audience to know that I am here for them. I also believe that NIA & THE NUMBERS GAME will help readers to make empowering choices. Enjoy reading NIA & THE NUMBERS GAME!

-Dr. Kela Henry

Acknowledgements

First, I must pay homage to my wonderful and supportive family. I am unbelievably blessed to be a part of such a loving, close-knit and rather functional family.

Although Daddy passed on to the loving arms of the Most High God before this work began, his positive energy imbued me with a sense of purpose to get it done. Mom, you were always excited about this book project from the moment I told you about it four years ago, and your enthusiasm never faded. Thanks for being in my corner.

To my sister Anetra, whose contributions both great and small helped to mold the final outcome—your critiques and keen eye helped me to clarify my message. Thanks for coming on this journey with me and always having my back (even when I probably got on your nerves).

To the rest of my family—I am eternally grateful for your love and encouragement. You all have told me over the years how proud of me you are, and with the completion of this book, I hope you'll be even prouder.

To Tara Pringle Jefferson and Aja Dorsey Jackson for their contributions to this book.

To Friendship Baptist Church—thank you for being my surrogate family and my church home. I felt comfortable from the moment I walked into the sanctuary ten years ago. I truly appreciate all the support given to me during this process whether it was with prayers, participation with the video shoot, or kind words.

To Haywood Smith, who met with me very early on and gave me valuable information. An accomplished author, I value her wit, insight and experience. She made me feel like I could do this in the same way that a great sports coach makes a player feel more confident and helps them to believe that they can!

Last, but certainly not least, to Denise Marsa, who planted the seed four years ago and has been walking by my side, figuratively speaking, ever since. From NYC to Atlanta—all those brainstorming phone sessions have paid off.

Chapter One: 4 - 1 = 3 + 3, a New Family Dynamic

Nia Ferguson flinched when the sound of banging pots from the kitchen came through her bedroom door. Her parents were having an argument. Again.

Her father's voice came at full volume. "Sabrina, I never see you anymore! You're never home! Always at work or at school or at the nursing home with your father. You never have time for us!" Nia's dad Paul complained bitterly to his wife.

A cabinet door slammed, then her mother's voice said "Dammit, Paul! I'm getting my R.N. as fast as I can so I can earn more. We still owe twelve thousand dollars on the credit cards from when you were out of work. I'm trying to do my part to get those paid off, but it doesn't seem like you appreciate that." Her voice was harsh. "As for Daddy, what am I supposed to do? Just let him die in that place? Sammy and Sherita and Sheldon say they'll help, but then always have some excuse not to."

Paul drew a sharp breath. "So stand up to them! He's their father too! Make them take care of your dad for a bit. They have more time than you do."

"I've tried and you know it!" her mother shot back.

"Nia needs you!" her father countered.

The sound of her name made Nia feel sick to her stomach. She hated being dragged into this.

"She's only twelve, and you know how it gets for girls at that age these days. So many bad things can happen. She needs a mother who's around more often."

What Nia needed was for them to stop fighting.

"I'm doing the best I can," Sabrina replied, turning her attention to the dishes in the sink. "I'm trying. It's great that you finally have a new job, but every time I turn around there's another unexpected expense. And you don't seem to appreciate what I'm sacrificing here!"

"I do," her father said. "But something's got to change around here."

Nia couldn't help feeling guilty. She'd needed new clothes the week before because she'd outgrown her others. And PJ had fallen off the merry-go-round at the park when she was pushing it, and he'd had to get stitches in his chin at the emergency room.

"This isn't going to be forever," her mother argued. "Just until I finish school and get a decent job."

"It's already taken three times longer than you said at first," her father said. Then his voice went weary. "Sabrina, we can't go on like this. *I* can't go on like this."

Nia stopped breathing. What did he mean? He'd never said that before.

On and on her parents went, their voices rising and falling for what seemed like hours. Nia shoved her homework aside, curled up on her bed and tried to block out the noise by putting a pillow over her head. *I wonder when they'll get tired,* she thought to herself as her eyelids got heavy. Minutes later, she was asleep.

***

That was a year ago. One week after the big blow up argument, Nia's dad had moved out, kissing her on the forehead and telling her he wasn't going far. This was true. He'd found an apartment three blocks away that was on the way to Nia's school.

Since then, Nia had been adjusting to life in two homes. She kept leaving things with one parent and forgetting to bring them "home" to the other. She'd get confused about which parent she'd see on which days and when she woke up some mornings, she wasn't quite sure where she was. It felt strange to be at her dad's place without her mom also joining them at the table for breakfast. Her younger brother, PJ, was only six, so he enjoyed having toys in two different places and getting a new whole bedroom at his dad's place. He didn't quite understand what was going on. Nia and PJ especially looked forward to their regular family dates at the local bowling alley. That was something their family had always done together, and their father made sure to keep the tradition going, although now it was a threesome instead of a foursome.

Even though Nia knew her parents hadn't been getting along so well, their separation was still a shock. She thought her parents might still get back together, but in the meantime she had to face the fact that they were living apart, and it was causing a lot of stress.

Nia was a little worried about her mom. Every time Nia saw her, she was hunched over the dining room table, flipping through bills and letting out loud sighs. Now that her parents were divorcing, Nia's mom felt trapped at work. She worked as a medical assistant in a busy office, and money was always tight. Her schoolwork became even more important as she needed to get a better job. "Remember, my Nia," her mom always told her, "your education can take you places beyond your wildest dreams. Keep your head in those books."

Not that Nia had a choice! Both of her parents were strict when it came to school. Her parents gave her a simple phone—not the latest like some of her friends had—to have in case anything came up while she was watching PJ. They let her use it to call or text her friends as long as she got A's and B's. Anything less than that meant she would lose her phone until her grades got back up. And even though her parents didn't live together anymore, they both still asked her about homework, and kept up with her grades just like they did when they were all under one roof.

For the most part, Nia was happy. Even though her parents had broken up, they didn't fight anymore which meant a lot more peace and quiet at home. School was cool, as she was enjoying seventh grade. Her best friends April and Patrice were in her homeroom, and it was great seeing them every day. Her biggest challenge was figuring out how to navigate this new world where the boys suddenly started trying to get girls' attention, wearing too much body spray and not enough deodorant. This one boy in particular, Brandon, was always in Nia's face. He was shorter than most of the boys their age, the last one to hit his growth spurt. His face was round and chubby, and he spent too much time in class talking and asking the teacher goofy questions. He was nice to Nia, even when he was teasing her.

"Hey, Nia," Brandon said one day in math class, tapping her on her back. "I can't see the board." That day, her curly fro was in a twist-out and was as wide as her shoulders. Nia loved when her hair was big and full.

"Then move to another seat," Nia said quietly, smiling sweetly.

"But I don't want to," Brandon whispered, smiling back.

Nia shrugged and turned back to face the board and finish up her math problems. Five seconds later, Brandon tapped her on the back again.

"What?"

"What are you doing after school today?"

"I don't know. Studying probably. We have that big test tomorrow, remember?"

"Oh, that's right," Brandon said. He leaned back in his seat and shook his head. "You're smart. You don't need to study. Come with me to Chipotle instead."

"Boy, what?"

"My brother works there. He gets me free food all the time," Brandon whispered.

"That's nice," Nia replied. She kept working on her paper.

"I can get you a burrito," Brandon said.

"A what?"

"A burrito. 'Cause you're nice to me all the time."

"Even when you can't see because of me?"

"Yeah," he said, laughing.

Just then, their teacher Ms. Irving looked up and spotted the two of them talking. "I take it you two must be done with your work if you have time to talk, right?"

"I finished five minutes ago, Ms. Irving," Brandon said proudly. "You want to see my paper?"

Nia tried not to laugh as Brandon got up to show Ms. Irving his work and turned her attention back to her geometry paper. Brandon was right – she didn't *need* to study because she was incredibly gifted when it came to math problems. She loved how she felt after she finished a really hard problem, like there wasn't anything she couldn't do.

She was almost done with her paper when she felt that all-too familiar trickle in her pants. *Oh no,* she thought. *Not today.*

"Ms. Irving, may I go to the bathroom?"

"Yes, but hurry right back. We'll be moving on to the next lesson soon."

Nia grabbed her book bag and scurried to the bathroom. Sure enough, her period had started and caught her off guard. She dug in her bag for the pads she kept and groaned when she realized she was out.

She sat in the stall for a minute, unsure of what to do, when she heard the bathroom door open and close. In came the familiar *tap-tap-tap* of Ms. Jimenez's high heels. Ms. Jimenez was the art teacher and had started at the school just last year after moving to Atlanta from the Dominican Republic.

She quickly became one of Nia's favorites. Nia always wondered how she could stand all day in those shoes and not get paint on them.

Should I ask her for help? Nia wondered. *It could be embarrassing.*

Nia knew her only other option was to ball up some tissue as a makeshift pad until she could ask the school nurse.

The nurse should have some, right?

Nia decided to just ask. They were both girls, right?

Nia waited until Ms. Jimenez came out of the stall. Nia saw Ms. Jimenez's high heels under the door as she walked past Nia's stall toward the sink.

"Um…Ms. Jimenez?" Nia called out.

Ms. Jimenez turned toward the stall and bent down. "Is that you, Nia?" she asked. Her warm accent floated under the door and began to make Nia feel more comfortable, now that she had someone there to help.

"It's me," she said. "I…um…was wondering if you have an extra pad with you? I need one."

"Hmm, okay." Nia heard what sounded like Ms. Jimenez unzipping her purse and rummaging around. "Let's see what I have here...I have a tampon. Do you use tampons, Nia?"

"No, not yet."

"That's okay. Here, I found a pad! I usually carry one in case you girls need it." Ms. Jimenez bent down and held the pad under the door.

Nia got a good look at her shoes today – cherry red sling backs, with not a drop of paint on them!

"Thank you, Ms. Jimenez."

"Of course! We have to look out for each other, don't we? I'll see you a little later on," Ms. Jimenez replied, and Nia heard the bathroom door shut behind her.

Five minutes later, Nia slipped back into geometry, feeling embarrassed and making a mental note to put more pads in her book bag so she wouldn't be caught off guard again. *So glad I wore dark pants today,* Nia thought. *Whew.*

Let's Talk

If you're a teen like Nia, you might be wondering how anyone expects you to navigate becoming an adolescent. There's so much coming at you that it's hard to wrap your head around it. Your body is changing, your friends are changing, and you might even have family issues like Nia does.

The beauty of this time in your life is that you are developing into the person you are meant to be. You're learning about what you like and don't like, and what your gifts and talents are. This is a perfect time for you to focus on yourself and determine how you want to show yourself to the world. In the pages that follow, we'll walk together to help you figure out how to make the most of your teen years.

Periods

It can be a (literal) pain, but getting your period simply means your body is joining the ranks of millions of girls and women before you.

Nothing about menstruation is shameful or anything to be embarrassed about.

It might be awkward to talk about it in front of boys or your parents but trust me—it's a completely natural part of being female.

In previous generations, having your period wasn't something that was discussed openly.

It was almost like joining a secret society, where no one spoke about the rules or what they experienced. It is only recently that having your period is now seen as a normal bodily function, something we do just because our bodies are primed to do it!

So why do we menstruate? The simplest explanation for the arrival of our first period means our bodies are capable of becoming pregnant. Each month, your body releases an egg into your fallopian tubes and it travels down to your uterus. If no sperm is there to fertilize the egg, the uterus will shed its lining (the now-unnecessary cushion for the fertilized egg). That is the blood you see when you go to the bathroom. On average, this cycle will take anywhere from twenty-four to thirty days to complete. Your period will last anywhere from three to seven days, with most ladies reporting their heaviest "flow" during the first few days.

For most girls, having your period is pretty basic but for others, it comes with a few issues. These may include:

- cramping
- nausea/vomiting
- diarrhea or constipation
- fatigue
- breast soreness
- bloating
- acne
- headaches
- changes in mood
- changes in appetite

With a list like that you might be wondering, *How long will I have to put up with my period?!* The beautiful thing is that once you understand the symptoms around your period, you'll be better equipped to make sure you're comfortable.

The first thing I recommend is for teens to track their periods. It might take a few years before your period becomes regular or predictable, but the only way to make an accurate guess is to keep track when it comes. You can use a wall calendar or planner, or you can use a free app like Glow or PeriodTracker. Both help you track when your period is coming and how long it lasts, but they also help you track your symptoms. Over time you will begin to notice patterns, for example, you might always get really tired a week before your period arrives. It can also help you be prepared with pads, tampons or cups (more on those later!) so you're not caught off guard like Nia was.

What Should You Use?

Way back in the day, period products were these bulky contraptions that included a belt (yes!) around your waist. Now we have period underwear that allows you to go without a tampon or a pad at all. But how do you know which products are right for you?

The table below gives you all of your options, along with the pros and cons of each:

	Pads	Tampons	Menstrual Cups	Period Underwear
Pros	Easy to use and give a sense of protection (there are also washable cloth varieties for women who want to be eco-friendly)	Discreet; can use while swimming	Discreet; can use while swimming; no irritants; washable	Discreet; no odor; washable
Cons	Can feel a little bulky; must change every three to four hours	Takes a little practice with insertion; small risk of Toxic Shock Syndrome*	Can be messy to remove; cleanup might not be possible in public areas	Might still cause anxiety while wearing them
Cost	Relatively inexpensive	Relatively inexpensive	$10-$30 depending on brand (but you only need one–two!)	$12-$30

*A rare but serious condition caused by a bacterial infection

Easing the pain

Most over-the-counter pain relievers like Advil or Aleve will do the job on period pain, but whatever pain reliever you take, it's important to manage the pain and your cramps.

Begin taking medication at the first sign of your period and follow the instructions for the appropriate dosage. You don't want to stop and let your period cramps come roaring back. A warm heating pad can also help.

But if you find your period pains are too severe and they limit your day-to-day activities, it's a good time to ask your parent or guardian to take you to the doctor so they can make them more manageable. Often doctors will prescribe medication to help alleviate some of your most uncomfortable symptoms.

All in all, having your period is a part of life that is easier to manage as time goes on and you have a better sense of your cycle. Like Nia showed when she asked Ms. Jimenez for a pad, there is nothing to be ashamed of. It's your body's way of saying, "We're growing up!"

"I Think He Likes Me!"

Perhaps you have someone in your class like Brandon — always teasing you or somehow in your face, trying to talk to you. You might not even understand some of the ways your body reacts to this attention. What do you do? How should you respond? It can feel so complicated!

The great news is that you have a long time to get it right when it comes to crushes.

As we said earlier in the book, your teen years are the time for you to figure out who you are and that includes who you like and don't like.

At this age, everyone is trying to figure it out. So don't feel pressured if your friends all have girlfriends or boyfriends and you feel a little left out. Trust me—they feel just as confused as you do. And how could they not? This is new to everyone.

But not all crushes are fun. If you like someone and you find out they don't like you in the same way, it can hurt. But it won't hurt forever.

What you see on TV, or maybe even in your school—fighting over boys, worrying too much if a boy likes you—can give you conflicting ideas about how you handle this new stage in your life. Should you be upfront and tell a boy you like him? Should you wait until he talks to you? What if he likes another girl — should you stop being friends with her?

What's most important is to simply be you. There's no need to act like anybody else to get someone to like you. It can be tempting to say you like basketball because your crush likes basketball, but if you don't care about Stephen Curry or any other NBA player, it's okay to own that. Whoever likes you has to like the true you, not the person you pretend to be. Be kind and considerate, but remember that your comfort level is more important than a boy's feelings. Don't feel pressured to bend your boundaries just because you're afraid to hurt someone's feelings.

The second important thing is not to take it so seriously. At this age, having crushes and liking some of your classmates is supposed to be fun! It's nice to have someone to hang out with and talk to without having so much pressure to make a relationship last.

Also remember that this is the age when your grades begin to matter most. What you do in middle school can predict how you'll perform in high school, which in turn can predict how well you'll do in college. That's why it's important to remember that school is the priority and boys are just people to have fun with.

As one of the featured speakers at *Glamour's* 2015 "The Power of an Educated Girl" event, former First Lady Michelle Obama said it best: "There is no boy, at this age, cute enough or interesting enough to stop you from getting an education. If I had worried about who liked me and who thought I was cute when I was your age, I wouldn't be married to the President of the United States today."

What You Should Know —Your Menstrual Cycle
Quiz –Can You Answer These True or False Questions?

1. Tampons can't get lost in the vagina. T F
2. If you have any discharge from your vagina, you should go to the doctor immediately. T F
3. Using scented soaps and perfumes in your genital area is a good way to smell clean. T F
4. Your period should come every 28 days. T F
5. Tampons will hurt when you insert them. T F
6. It's better to use a pad at night versus a tampon. T F
7. Using a tampon means you're no longer a virgin. T F

Answer Key:

1. **True.** Tampons sit comfortably nestled in the vagina and can't pass through your cervix, which sits at the end of your vagina. It

acts like a stopper and keeps the tampon from going any further. If you feel like your tampon is stuck or you can't find it, have confidence that it's not floating anywhere else in your body.

2. **False.** Discharge (clear or light colored) is a normal part of how your vagina works. Discharge is fluid that cleans away bacteria and keeps your vagina clean. However, if your discharge is yellow, green or otherwise abnormal in color or texture, it might be a sign of a vaginal infection and you should see a doctor.
3. **False.** When you clean yourself, be sure to use only a gentle soap with no added fragrances or dyes, and don't allow any to enter your vagina (be sure to rinse very well!). Using scented soaps sounds like a good idea, but those products are too harsh for your vagina and can cause irritation and infection.
4. **False.** Menstruation cycles vary from person to person, particularly when you are first starting out.
5. **False** (kinda). Tampons should not hurt, but if you are a bit frightened by the thought of using them they might be uncomfortable to insert, and it might take a little practice before you get the hang of it.
6. **True.** Most doctors recommend using a pad at night to lower the risk of toxic shock syndrome. (Using a tampon for longer than 8 hours increases your risk.)
7. **False.** What you use during your period has no impact on your virginity. Your hymen may break if you use tampons or menstrual cups, but it can also break during sports, exercise or just day to day life. No worries.

Chapter Two: 1 Mistake, Busted

Two Years Later

Nia scooped up her books and papers and stuffed them into her book bag. The final bell of the day had just rung, and she was ready to go home. A few months into ninth grade, Nia thought high school was so much harder than middle school. More papers, more tests, more homework. She was looking forward to giving her brain a break for a little while once she got home, and before she had to get PJ off of the bus and start her homework.

Nia filed out into the hallway and made it to her locker the same time as April, her best friend since third grade. They had morning classes together but none in the afternoon, so it felt like forever since they'd last seen each other.

"Girl, guess what?" April said as she dumped her books in the locker next to Nia's.

"What?"

"No, you need to guess!"

Nia rolled her eyes. April was always so dramatic about everything. This guessing game could be about anything. "I don't know, April. You gotta give me a clue at least."

"It's about your boyfriend, Brandon," April whispered.

"He's not my boyfriend!"

"Girl, please. He might as well be. All he does is follow you around and tell you those corny jokes."

"Leave him alone," Nia said, laughing and slipping her book bag on her shoulder. "He's nice, though."

"Yeah, he *is* nice," April agreed. "And he's cute too."

Nia and April had spent many days texting about all the ways the boys seemed to have changed overnight. In elementary school, boys were always off in their own groups, playing basketball and watching movies, but as soon as middle school hit, it was like they couldn't get enough of the opposite sex. It definitely didn't stop now that they were in high school. Nia and April didn't quite know how to respond to this new attention, so they leaned on each other to try to figure it out.

They got a lot of advice from Nia's friend, Patrice. They'd become friends after she moved to their district in sixth grade, and Patrice was always slightly ahead of Nia in terms of checking off milestones. She got her period first, began to get boobs first, and now in high school, Patrice was the only one out of the three to have a boyfriend. She had been going out with Marcus since the beginning of the school year, even though the most they had done was go to the mall together. Patrice had waited patiently at Foot Locker while Marcus looked at all the shoes he couldn't yet afford. She'd told Nia that she had wondered what the point was of $200 shoes that you couldn't really wear or get dirty, but if she had learned anything from her three older sisters, it was not to question boys' love for sneakers.

Right on cue, Patrice came sashaying down the hall, flaunting her new short haircut. She changed her hair every three weeks or so, thanks to her older sister who was a hairstylist in Buckhead.

"What up, Nia-bia?" Patrice said, turning then to look at April. "April, girl, you look like you got a secret to tell."

"I've been trying to get her to tell me for the past five minutes," Nia said, poking April in the shoulder.

April waved her hands as if to say it was too noisy in the hallway. "Come outside and I'll tell you."

The three girls slipped out the side door and into the bright fall light. Even though it was October, it was still warm enough for students to be congregating outside, killing time before they went home. The trio walked over to the green bench beside the football field and took a seat.

"So what is it?" Nia said, getting impatient.

"Well..." April looked around to make sure no one else was paying attention to them. Nia rolled her eyes at her dramatic friend.

"I heard Brandon was going to be switching schools soon," she whispered.

"Girl, what?" Patrice said, waving her hand. "That's not gossip!"

"Yes, it is," April said, cuddling up to Nia in an imitation of Brandon. "Because Nia's going to miss her Brandon-boo."

"Whatever," Nia said, laughing and playfully shoving April upright. "When did you hear that?"

"Earlier today. Brandon's older brother was talking about how they are going to be moving soon and they won't be in our district after winter break," April said.

"That's sad, though," Patrice said. "I'd hate if Marcus moved away."

"Marcus is your boyfriend, though," Nia pointed out. "Brandon is just...a boy in my class."

Patrice and April rolled their eyes simultaneously. "It's okay to admit you like him," Patrice urged Nia. "Go on, admit it!"

"I don't like him like that," Nia said. "I mean...not really."

"He's too short," Patrice said. "I think I'm taller than he is."

"He's not that short," Nia said. "He got taller this summer."

Patrice raised her eyebrows. "It's okay to admit you like him," she repeated. "I won't tell anybody."

Nia shook her head and stood up to leave. She heaved her book bag over one shoulder and turned to face her friends. "I gotta get going so I can be there when my little brother gets off the bus. I'll see y'all tomorrow?"

"Wait!" April said. She popped up off the bench and pulled her phone out of her pocket. "You didn't tell us what you were going to wear to the game on Friday." April pulled up a photo of a woman wearing a striped blue dress and showed it to her friends. "My mom said she'd take me to the mall tomorrow to see if I can get one."

Bobby D, the twenty-two-year-old rapper who had graduated from their school just a few years earlier, was now one of the hottest in the game. As part of his "Homecoming" tour, he was going around to perform at Atlanta high schools all month long. He had given $10,000 to their school and was coming to perform at halftime at Friday's football game. The school was going to use the contribution to create a new Science, Technology, Engineering and Math program.

Nia, being one of the top math and science students, had been selected to go to a meet-and-greet before his performance. Nia was nervous, as Bobby was one of her favorite rappers and she couldn't wait to get a picture with him.

"I don't know what I'm wearing yet," Nia said. "Can I come with you to the mall?" She knew she would have a little time before she had to pick up PJ the next day because their mom's friend, who lived a block over, picked him up from school a few days a week to let him play with her twin boys for a few hours.

"I don't think my mom would mind," April said, handing the phone to Patrice.

"You gotta come home with me though because I don't think my mom wants to drive out of the way to pick you up from your house."

Patrice squinted at the photo. "You will be doing the most if you get that outfit."

"What?" April turned the phone around to look at the outfit again. "It's cute! And it's perfect for the game."

"You can't look so thirsty," Patrice replied, rolling her eyes.

"What's thirsty about looking cute?"

"Nothing," Patrice said, waving her hand. "Wear what you want, girl. I'm just gonna wear some jeans and a cute tee. Not going through all that trouble to look super cute for Bobby D when we are just gonna be faces in the crowd." She poked Nia's shoulder. "Not like the superstar over here who gets to be his girl for the day."

"Whatever," Nia said, laughing. "I wish, though!"

They hugged and parted ways, each headed home for an afternoon of studying.

Nia was about done with her practice math test when her phone buzzed. It was Brandon. She had almost forgotten that she had given him her number.

These days, Nia kept her phone off most of the time because she didn't want her friends to see her still using a cheap phone that came out almost three years prior while everyone else had the latest model. Her parents still felt like she only needed the phone for emergencies.

Outside of anything that might come up while she was watching PJ, going back and forth to school or doing activities with her friends, they thought all the extras were unnecessary and outside of their budget, so Nia couldn't do much more than make a phone call and send a limited number of texts.

When Brandon texted her, she was curious as to what he wanted: *Wyd?* he asked.

Ugh, Nia thought. She hated when boys had to abbreviate everything: *Just got done studying*, she texted back.

He replied: *Me 2. Can I come over?*

Nia froze. *Have him come over to my house?* She thought. *I don't know....*

Even though she denied it in front of her friends, Nia really did like Brandon. He was always doing nice things for her like buying her cookies from the vending machine because he remembered how much she said she liked chocolate chip or complimenting her when she felt like she was having a bad hair day.

Plus, he'd had a small growth spurt since middle school and he was no longer at her neck but now was eye-to-eye with her. His face had lost a bit of its boyish look, and he was now looking more like someone she could actually date, although dating wasn't going to be in the cards for her for a while. Her parents were very strict and agreed that Nia shouldn't be dating until she was sixteen. Nia thought that was unfair but she didn't want to push the issue. She figured she'd wait a couple months and try again.

But now Brandon wanted to come over.

Nia thought for a minute. Today, like most days, she was home alone with her brother PJ. She was responsible for watching him after school until her mom got home at 5:30. He was only eight and was very likely to blab that Nia had a boy over, but Nia thought maybe she could bribe him to be quiet.

Nia texted Brandon her address. He said he'd be there in five minutes.

"Hey, PJ." Nia tapped on her brother's door. He was playing a video game and had his back to his sister. "PJ!"

He jumped and turned to look at her. "You scared me!"

"I'm sorry," she said softly.

She looked out the window, as if Brandon had somehow managed to get to her house already. "Hey, do me a favor."

"What is it?" PJ frowned. He didn't like getting bossed around.

"A friend of mine is about to come over," she said carefully and then she paused.

"So I need you to not tell Mom. And *definitely* don't tell Dad."

"Why would I tell Mom?" he asked. "Mom doesn't care if your friends come over. Is it April? I like April. I don't like Patrice. She talks too much."

"No, it's not April. Or Patrice."

"Then who is it?"

"It's another one of my friends, PJ. Just...stay up here, okay? If you do this for me, I will buy you a new video game."

PJ's eyes got wide. "Okay!"

That was easy, Nia thought as she left the room.

***

Ten minutes later, Brandon knocked on the front door.

Nia took a deep breath and swung the door open wide. "Hi, Brandon," she said quietly. She hustled him inside before all the neighbors could see who was visiting. Her neighbors, particularly Mr. Ivey, could be a nosy bunch.

"Your house is nice," he said, looking around at the small living room. A brown leather sofa was tucked into one corner, with a tan loveseat, a bit worn from age, sitting diagonally across from it. The walls were adorned with family photos and colorful black art pieces. Nia's mom loved art and would save up for a piece of art in the same way that other women collected purses. It was almost like she couldn't stand to see a bare wall anywhere in her house.

"Thanks," Nia said. She sat on the sofa and tucked her feet under her legs. "So what's up?"

"Nothing," Brandon said. "I didn't get to talk to you at school today so...I wanted to come by to see you."

Nia blushed. "Why did you want to see me?"

"I mean, you're cool," he said, slipping onto the cushion next to Nia.

"What does that even mean?" Nia smiled and leaned back on the couch.

"It means...you know...you're not like the other girls," Brandon finally said.

"And what does that mean?"

"You're nicer than a lot of the other girls. You don't crack jokes about how short I am. If I try to show you a funny video or something, you don't ignore me," he said.

"Well, that's rude," Nia said. "Girls do that?"

"All the time," he said. He leaned back on the couch cushions and turned to face Nia.

He switched topics quickly. "I know April probably told you."

"Told me what?"

"That I'm leaving soon. My dad got a new job so we're moving at the end of December."

Brandon looked sad and now that Nia knew for sure he was leaving, she was sad too.

"That sucks," she said, running her hands through her hair, a nervous habit she was trying to break.

"Yeah, I know. I don't really want to move but since I'm only a freshman, my parents think it'll be easy for me to start over someplace else."

"Are you worried about that? Making new friends and stuff?"

"A little," Brandon admitted. "But I'll miss you the most, I think."

Nia smiled so hard that both her dimples popped in. "Aww. Well, you can still text me. I'll be here."

Brandon slid a little closer to Nia and slipped his hand around her hip. "Are you going to miss me?"

Nia could smell every spritz of his AXE body spray and it overwhelmed her. But still, his body heat felt nice and she loved how heavy his hand felt on her side. "Yeah, I'll miss you. Of course."

Brandon smiled and leaned forward to kiss her on the cheek. Nia felt a hot flash go through her body and she froze. Brandon kissed her again—this time on her lips.

"Nia!" PJ called from upstairs.

"What!" Nia yelled. Brandon jumped, startled. She was angry that she had *finally* gotten to kiss a boy and her brother had to go ruin it. *There's no way I'm getting him his video game now.* "I…have to go see what he needs." Nia excused herself and ran upstairs.

"PJ! I told you I had a friend over!" Nia barged in her brother's room.

"Sorry," PJ mumbled. "The game froze and I just wanted you to fix it."

"Ugh, PJ," Nia fussed. She bent down to turn off the console and clicked the button again to turn it back on. "That's all you have to do. Turn it off and on again. It'll reset."

But Nia was still looking at the frozen screen. "Hmm. That's weird."

"I told you!" PJ said. "I know how to do it but that didn't work for me."

"Well, let's unplug it then," Nia said. "We have to hurry up because I told you I have company and I can't leave him downstairs by himself."

"You've got a *boy* over?" PJ squealed. "I'm telling Mommy! I'm telling Mommy!"

"Stop it!" Nia said. She clamped a hand over his mouth. "I thought I said that you couldn't tell Mom."

"I don't need a new video game," he said, gesturing to his pile of games beside the TV stand. "I haven't even played the ones Grandma got me for Christmas."

Nia opened her mouth to try to bargain again, but she was interrupted by a yell from the living room. "Nia!"

Her mom was home. Early.

***

Nia expected her mom to yell at her when she got home and found Brandon in the living room, but instead she gave Nia the silent treatment from the time she sent Brandon home all through dinner. PJ just ate his food quickly and slipped back upstairs so he wouldn't be caught in the crossfire. Nia knew something bad was brewing and tried to plead her case before her mom could really get going.

"Mom, it wasn't that bad," Nia insisted. "I didn't do anything wrong."

"I talked to your father," Nia's mom said instead, choosing to begin her own conversation. She rinsed off a plate, then stuck it in the bottom rack of the dishwasher. "He's not happy with you right now."

"I swear I didn't do anything with Brandon!" Nia argued. "We're just friends. He came over to see me and tell me that he's not going to be going to my school anymore."

Her mom didn't reply, and just kept placing more cups and plates in the dishwasher. She closed it and turned it on. The kitchen filled with the soft gentle hum.

Nia's mom picked up a dish towel and dried her hands. She was quiet and Nia knew that meant she was thinking of what to say.

Nia already had a pretty good idea of what the lecture was going to sound like. Nia had been born at the beginning of her mother's sophomore year of college. She had fully intended on continuing with school and graduating in two more years, but the pressures of school and motherhood proved to be too much. She left during spring semester of her sophomore year and concentrated full-time on raising her daughter. Ever since Nia was a little girl, she heard about how men lead to babies and babies lead to dreams deferred. She would insist that she was grateful for Nia and PJ, and that they were the reason she was back in school now, but Nia knew that she wished she had waited to be a mom. Nia expected this conversation to be more of the same.

Nia's mom sighed and motioned for Nia to sit at the kitchen table. "Okay, let's talk."

Nia tensed up. *What was this? She wanted to talk? About what? I already told her everything.*

"So you're growing up," her mom said, obviously choosing her words very carefully. "I know that. I can't wish you were a little girl forever because clearly you're getting older." She sighed again. "Did you and Brandon do anything before I came home? Tell me honestly, Nia."

"We just kissed. Once. That's it!"

"On the cheek or on the lips?"

"Lips," Nia said softly.

Her mom nodded. "Okay. And nothing else?"

"Nothing. PJ had called for me and I ran up to see what he needed because I knew I was supposed to be watching him so…"

Nia's mom put her hand up to stop Nia's rambling. "I believe you. Thank you for being honest with me."

Nia relaxed in her chair. "Okay."

"So you like this boy, Brandon?"

"I mean...he's okay," Nia said.

"I know what 'okay' means," her mom said. "And it's okay to have a crush on a boy and hope he likes you. But you know the rules. No boys over here when I'm not home."

"Yes, ma'am," Nia said softly.

"So you do understand that you are grounded, right? For the next two weeks."

Nia looked up at her mom, surprised at how calm she was being. She had imagined her mother would yell and get angry. But this was different.

"But the game is on Friday," she reminded her mom. "With Bobby D? I get to go backstage, remember?"

"Oh yes, I remember," her mom said calmly. "It's too bad that you can't go now, isn't it?"

Tears welled up in Nia's eyes. "But Mom!"

"All of our actions have consequences, Nia," her mom replied. "All of them. And it's up to you to remember that. I know you were looking forward to the game but that's the cost."

"But..." Nia began to plead.

Her mom held up her hand again and pushed back from the table. "You're a smart girl, Nia," she said. "And I know you are exploring what it means to be fifteen. All I ask is that you take your time. There's no rush on all of this. You have years and years to have crushes on boys and wonder if they like you just as much as you like them. Just take your time, okay?"

Let's Talk

Have you ever had an experience like this?

You get in trouble with your parents and you're not quite sure what to expect?

Nia expected her mom to get angry and yell because she had a boy at the house before she got home, but her reaction surprised her.

Nia's mom chose to use that opportunity to instead remind her daughter of the rules, talk to her about her feelings, and hand out the appropriate punishment.

Quite different from Nia's expectations, right?

As a teen, it's hard to gauge what your parents' reaction will be when you make a mistake. Often, you tend to think the worst of your parents' temper and anger, assuming they will fly off the handle, or worse, stop loving you in the same way they once did.

However, for most parents, they have been in your shoes and they remember what it's like to be a teenager. They remember having crushes on classmates and wanting to explore their boundaries.

But they also remember some of the consequences. They've been through what you're going through and they know what's on the other side, which is why they worry so much and set up rules to keep you from possibly experiencing some of the same consequences.

As a doctor, I tell my teen patients that their parents want the best for them. I have seen this to be true time and time again in my medical practice. Parents sit up all night worried about their children and they bring some of that worry into my office.

The best thing for you to do is to remember that your parents are on your side. It may not feel like it at times, but trust me they are working to make sure that you make it to adulthood fully independent and unencumbered with diseases or unplanned pregnancies or anything else that could derail your goals.

What You Should Know – Talking With Your Parents

These are the years where your relationship with your parents may change a bit. You want to be more independent, make your own decisions and feel like pulling away from your parents. Guess what? That is *normal.* Your parents know it's normal too. Here's my advice on building a strong relationship with your parents.

Be Honest

It's easy to think that you don't have to be truthful with your parents. What they don't know won't hurt them, right? But eventually, the truth comes to light and it makes things much more complicated than if you had been honest from the beginning. Do yourself a favor and make sure your parents can trust your word. If you think about it, this helps you more than it helps them. If someone is lying about you and your parents ask you about it, you want to be confident that they will believe you. That can't happen if you have a history of fudging the truth.

Be Respectful

Raising children can be hard work and parents don't always get it right. Just like this is your first time being a teenager, this is their first time raising you through this time period. Even if you feel like some of their rules are unfair, it's important to be respectful.

Ask Questions

Your parents should be there as a resource for you. If you have questions about something, ask them. Many teens hesitate because they don't want their parents to know they are thinking about sex or other "scary" topics.

But it's important that you have the answers to your questions so you are well informed and can make the best decisions. We'll talk more about this in a later chapter, with sample conversation starters to help you have more productive discussions with your parents in a way that's not so scary or intimidating.

Chapter Three: 1 More Mistake; Really in Trouble Now

Nia's father eased the car into park and looked over at his daughter in the passenger seat. "You ready?" he asked.

Nia bit her bottom lip and nodded.

Almost every Saturday morning since she'd turned sixteen, her father had taken her to a local elementary school parking lot to practice driving. He found some orange cones from the side of the building and set them up for her maneuverability practice.

"Cut the wheel, cut the wheel!" he would bellow from outside the car, watching as Nia inevitably turned the wheel in the wrong direction. "No, cut it the other way!"

After a few months of this early morning practice, Nia's dad began to let her drive on the street. The ten-minute drive from school to home was just far enough to give Nia a taste of what it was like to share the road with other drivers, but not too far or busy that she could run into any real trouble.

Now that she had mastered that quick drive, they'd been taking longer, more leisurely trips, where he could see how she handled merging in and out of thick Atlanta traffic.

"Okay, you know what to do," her dad said as they switched seats. He climbed in and shut the passenger door. "Ease it into drive and let's go."

"You're doing a great job," he said after a few minutes of driving. "Just get into the right lane and take it all the way home."

Her father seemed to relax a bit. He drummed his fingers on his knee and leaned forward to look out the window. "You okay?" he asked. "Nervous?"

"No," Nia said, shaking her head. She gripped the wheel and checked her rearview mirror. It was early, so traffic wasn't too congested this time of day.

"You're doing a great job," her dad said, patting her leg. "Just relax."

"You know Patrice took her driving test last week," Nia said.

"Did she? How'd she do?"

"She passed."

Her dad laughed. "Oh Lord, now I gotta worry about Patrice on the road? Jesus take the wheel."

Nia laughed too. "Yeah, remember when she hit the mailbox a couple months ago when she was practicing? I can't believe she passed."

"Well, if she passed then that means you will too."

"I better! I'm a way better driver," Nia said. "But Patrice got better. She's actually picking me up later to go to the movies."

"To the movies? With who?"

"Just me and Patrice."

He nodded. "To see what?"

"That new Spiderman movie."

"They just keep on making the same movie over and over again, don't they?" He shook his head. "How many times can you say the boy got bit by a spider and now he's strong?"

Nia turned the car onto her mom's street. She pulled up into the driveway and put the car in park. "How'd I do?"

"You did great. I'm proud of you." He unbuckled himself and got out of the car. He placed his hands on the roof of the car and smiled at his daughter. "I definitely think you'll pass this test. Maybe your mom will let you practice this week."

"I still get so nervous," Nia admitted.

"Ah, you'll be fine," he said, waving his hand. "You're *my* daughter and I only make winners." He winked and stood up straight. He looked toward the house. "Your mom home?"

"I think so," Nia said. She got out of the car and grabbed her purse from the backseat. "You want to go in and say hi to her?"

"No, I gotta run," he said. Nia tossed him the keys and he caught them, one-handed, with a smile. "But tell her I will call her later. I have to get PJ some new cleats for baseball, so we need to figure out when I can take him."

"Okay, Dad." Nia crossed the driveway to give him a hug. "Thanks for taking me driving today."

"Anytime, kid."

***

"Nia!" Patrice yelled for her friend and honked the horn. "We're going to be late!"

"Just a minute!" Nia fumbled with her keys and locked the door to the house. She fluffed her hair and ran over to where Patrice was waiting in her new car. Well, it was technically only new to Patrice but that didn't stop Patrice from bragging about it every chance she got.

"Why are you rushing me?" Nia asked as she clicked her seatbelt. "We've got plenty of time before the movie starts."

"You know I hate being late to things," Patrice replied, keeping her eyes on her mirrors as she backed out of the driveway.

"You just want to see Marcus," Nia teased.

Patrice smiled wide. "Well, yeah. I don't really care about the movie because we saw it last week already."

"You saw it already? Girl, we could have picked a different movie."

Patrice waved her hand. "It's fine. Gives me an excuse to get out of the house. My sisters have been driving me crazy. And I miss Marcus."

"You saw him two days ago!"

"I know," she said, smiling.

Nia pulled out her lip gloss, looking into the passenger side mirror while she applied it. "I can't believe you guys have been together so long."

"Yeah, I can't believe it either. That boy drives me crazy!" She laughed. "Did I tell you what he did on Wednesday?"

Patrice kept rambling about Marcus' latest stunt, and Nia half-listened as they drove to the movie theater. She was deep in her own thoughts until she heard Patrice say, "I'm thinking of finally giving him some next weekend."

"Wait, what? Doing it?"

"Well, my parents are going out of town and my sisters will be busy with their own lives so...next weekend would be perfect."

"I didn't know you two were talking about it," Nia said.

"I just think it's time, you know? We've been together for a while and I know he's ready. He's *been* ready."

"So you're gonna do it this weekend? Aren't you scared that it'll hurt?" Nia whispered.

"Why are you whispering?" Patrice laughed. "It's just us two in the car."

"But seriously, aren't you scared?"

"Of it hurting? No." Patrice shook her head.

"You know Shonda, Nikki's best friend? She said it hurt so bad! She hasn't tried it since."

"We'll go slow," Patrice said, and she winked at her friend. "After we do it, I'll report back and let you know if Shonda was right."

"Are you scared of getting pregnant?"

"Okay, what's with all the questions?" Patrice said. She glanced over at Nia. "You think I shouldn't do it?"

"I'm not saying that," Nia said, throwing up her hands. "I just didn't know you planned on doing it with Marcus."

Patrice nodded. "No, I'm not scared of getting pregnant. I took a few of my sister's condoms and I practiced putting one on a banana last week."

"No you didn't!"

"I did," Patrice said, laughing. "It's harder than it looks."

Nia thought back to all the times her mother warned her how sex equals babies. "You think you should get on birth control then? You know, in case the condom breaks?"

"You are *really* not trying to babysit my kids, huh?" Patrice joked.

Nia laughed and shook her head. "Not really."

"Alright, we're here." Patrice pulled into a spot and checked her lip gloss in the rearview mirror. "How do I look?"

"You look good, girl."

"So do you."

They grabbed their purses and headed over to the theater entrance where Brandon and Marcus were waiting. Suddenly, Patrice grabbed

Nia's arm and pulled her close. "Don't tell Brandon what I said about me and Marcus," she whispered in her ear.

***

Brandon grabbed Nia's hand and led her to the back row of seats. "Is this okay?" he asked, motioning for her to go in front of him to pick a seat. Even though it was a Saturday night, the theater was practically empty, save for a few other people scattered around the room. Nia and Brandon were the only ones in their row.

"Yeah, this is good." Nia plopped down into the middle seat and slid her purse off her shoulder. "Have you seen this movie before?"

"Nah, but Marcus said it was good so…." Brandon looked a few rows ahead where Patrice and Marcus were sitting. They were already kissing and groping each other before the lights went down.

Nia wondered if Brandon was thinking the same thing would happen between the two of them. They had been together for a few months but this was their first time going on an actual date. Mostly, they just hung out together after school and texted each other. So far, they had only kissed a little. A peck here, a peck there. Nia was nervous, but if she was honest with herself, she wouldn't mind doing a little kissing here in this theater either. Brandon was *cute*. He was no longer the chubby faced boy from seventh grade, but a handsome sophomore who also thought *she* was cute.

The lights went down and the first movie preview came up on the screen. Brandon leaned over and pulled some Sour Patch Kids out of his pocket. "You want some?" he whispered to Nia.

She held her hand out, then let the sour-sweet candy melt on her tongue. "Whew, this is sour!" she whispered back.

Brandon smiled and popped some in his mouth. "It's not too bad."

He slid his arm around her shoulders and she angled her body a bit to lean into him.

Brandon used his free hand to jiggle the armrest, pleased to discover that it could raise up out of the way. She put her head on his shoulder, laughing a bit at the movie previews, and they whispered to each other which movie they wanted to go see next.

From her spot in the back of the dark theater, Nia couldn't see much other than the back of Marcus' head as Patrice tried to devour his face. *That girl has no shame*, Nia thought, laughing a bit to herself.

Brandon must have been thinking the same thing because he leaned down a bit and whispered, "Patrice is about to get pregnant."

"Shut up," Nia said jokingly. "They're just...kissing."

They looked at each other for a moment, and almost simultaneously leaned forward, their lips meeting softly. Brandon gently tilted Nia's face toward him and kissed her again. He slipped his hand around her back and pulled Nia closer to him.

Nia kissed him harder. For a moment, she forgot that they were in public and that this display of affection was unlike her. She had always been quiet and shy, a bit reserved when it came to boys, often unsure of how to respond or act. But *this*? She liked this.

She felt Brandon slip his hand under her shirt to fiddle with her bra hooks. She thought about stopping him, but everything felt so good that she was momentarily unable to speak. Brandon kissed her lips again, and then traced a path to her neck. She leaned back, giving him more access to her neck and rubbing his back as encouragement to keep going.

"Nia?"

A familiar voice broke Nia's concentration. She jumped, pulling down her shirt to cover her stomach. The light from the screen illuminated her neighbor, Mr. Ivey. He was holding hands with a woman, presumably his date, and standing next to them with a look of disapproval.

"Um, Mr. Ivey, hello," Nia whispered, her face flushing hot. Brandon sank down in his seat.

"I thought that was you," Mr. Ivey replied. He motioned for his date to scoot past Nia and Brandon to move toward their seats. "Good evening."

Nia didn't respond but instead wished desperately that she could somehow melt into the seat and disappear. *Please don't keep talking to me*, she thought to herself. *This is embarrassing enough as it is.*

Mr. Ivey took a seat with his date a few seats down from Nia and Brandon just as the movie finally started. Brandon leaned over. "Are you okay?"

Nia just shook her head and kept her eyes on the screen. Brandon tried to put his arm around her again, but Nia just shook her head again and kept looking forward. Brandon sighed, pulled out the rest of the candy from his pocket and ate in silence until the movie was over.

***

"I am so dead!" Nia said on the drive home with Patrice.

"You didn't do anything I wasn't doing," Patrice pointed out.

"That's not the point. *You* didn't get caught by your neighbor making out with your boyfriend."

"I sure didn't, because that would not go over well with my mama, I'll tell you that," she replied. "So what are you going to do?"

"I don't know," Nia admitted, biting her bottom lip.

"Well, you don't know for sure that he would tell your parents, right?"

"Right."

"So don't say anything. Wait to see if they mention something. If they don't, then you're good and you don't have to worry about it."

"But man, I think he will tell, though," Nia said. "You remember last year when my mom came home early and found Brandon in the living room?"

"Yeah?"

"Well, Mr. Ivey came over afterward and told her everything he knew—what time Brandon got there, what he was wearing, *everything*."

"Mr. Ivey's a snitch!" Patrice laughed.

"He is! That's why I'm freaking out. He didn't say anything to me but man, I gotta figure out what to do."

"You know my motto," Patrice said, "keep your mouth shut!"

"I can't believe I got caught up like that," Nia admitted.

"Because it felt good, that's why!" Patrice rolled her eyes. "You act like you had sex with him."

"I didn't but...I wanted to."

"But you didn't," Patrice reminded her, "so why are you beating yourself up?"

"Because I know if my parents find out I was all up in a theater with Brandon, and Mr. Ivey caught me with my bra almost off, that'll be it. No more Brandon. No more dates. No more boyfriends 'til I move out."

"That would suck," Patrice agreed. "So maybe you should just come clean first. That might help."

"You know what? Drop me off at my dad's," Nia said. "Mr. Ivey is probably at my mom's house right now telling all my business."

Nia pulled her phone out and texted her mom. *Headed to Dad's. I'll spend the night there. Be back tomorrow.*

A few minutes later, her mom responded. *Okay, sweetheart. See you then.*

Nia leaned back in the seat and closed her eyes. Her phone buzzed again. It was Brandon.

Sorry about what happened.

Nia sighed and quickly typed out a reply. *Not your fault.*

Her phone buzzed again. *I feel bad. Let me know what happens when u get home OK?*

Nia smiled. *I will.*

***

Nia closed the door behind her and set her purse on the table. Her father was in the kitchen, stirring a pot of what looked to be gumbo on the stove.

"Hey, Nia!" he said, looking surprised to see her. Nia normally didn't make a habit of dropping by unannounced, but he never turned down an opportunity to see his baby girl.

"What are you doing here?" he asked, wiping his hands on a kitchen towel and crossing the room to give her a hug.

Nia realized she didn't come up with an excuse in the car so she just winged it. "Patrice just dropped me off from the movies so I figured I'd come over here so, um, I could tell you how it was."

"Was it as stupid as I thought it would be?" he asked with a smile.

"Yeah, it was pretty dumb," Nia said. "Same old story, just a different guy playing Spiderman."

"I knew it. Hollywood has run out of ideas." He gestured to the stove. "I'm making gumbo—you want some?"

"Oh, of course. Yeah." Her dad's gumbo was practically world-famous. He'd entered it into festivals and food contests all over the city.

He had come in second at the Peachtree Cook Off last year and had been tinkering with the recipe ever since to get it to number one.

He dipped in a spoon to get a taste. "Hmm…just about done," he said, shaking a few drops of hot sauce and grabbing a wooden spoon to stir. He turned the heat down to low and put the lid back on the pot.

Nia took off her shoes and got settled on the stool next to the breakfast bar. She fiddled with her hands for a bit and couldn't quite seem to shake the feeling that something was about to go down.

"I'll be right back," her dad said. "Let me run upstairs for a minute." She could hear his heavy footsteps as he climbed the stairs.

Nia exhaled and tried to calm herself down. *It's fine,* she told herself. *I didn't do anything wrong. This isn't that bad.*

Just then, her dad's cell phone rang, interrupting her internal pep talk and her heart raced. Nia recognized the ringtone he set for her mom, and she was bracing herself for the worst.

"Hello?" she could hear her dad answer from the other room. "Hey, Sabrina, what's up?"

For the second time that night Nia wished she could just melt into the floor. *Why did I think coming over here would be better?*

She heard her dad get silent as her mom was inevitably telling her everything that Mr. Ivey had snitched. "Uh-huh," she heard him say. "And this was today?"

Nia tried to get her story straight and think of what she could possibly say to get out of this. But she drew a blank. *How, exactly, do you explain getting felt up in a theater and being so caught up that you don't even care who sees you?*

She kept her breath low and even and waited for her dad to talk to her.

"That was your mother," her dad said as he stood in the doorway.

Nia didn't speak.

"What is this your mom is telling me about you and Brandon?" he asked. He put his phone on the kitchen table and sat down, turning his chair so he could look directly at Nia. "I thought you went to the movies with Patrice."

"Patrice…and Brandon," she admitted.

"Yeah, I heard." He looked disappointed, and Nia hated feeling like he was judging her for being irresponsible. "So do you want to tell me what happened, or are we going to keep playing games?"

She took a deep breath. "I'm sorry."

"Sorry for what?"

"Sorry for not telling you that I was going to the movies with Brandon and then sorry for...everything else."

"And what is everything else?"

"Dad, this is uncomfortable, talking about this stuff with you."

He shook his head. "No, you decided to come over here rather than go to your mom's so guess what? You're talking about it with me. Spill it."

"Mr. Ivey caught us..." Nia struggled to finish.

"From what your mom told me, he caught you with your bra off," he finished.

"It was unhooked, but it wasn't off," she said, trying to make it seem less serious than it really was.

"So, that makes it better?" He rubbed his temples. "So, you went to the movies —without telling me or your mom that Brandon would be there —and then you got caught getting felt up and making out with your boyfriend. Is that what happened tonight?"

Nia just nodded.

Her dad let this information soak in a bit. He tapped his fingers on the table and turned again to face his daughter.

"Your mother thinks that you and Brandon need to take a break," he said slowly. "And I have to say that I agree with her."

"You want me to break up with him?" Nia couldn't believe what she was hearing.

"Yes, we both think it's better if you two cool out for a while," he said. "We don't want you getting distracted and stunts like this make us feel like you are beginning to lose focus on what's really important."

"But my grades are good," Nia pointed out. "I'm still doing well in all my classes...this is just one mistake."

"Yes, but you are getting older and everything matters a bit more," he replied. "You are a sophomore now and while you think you have all the time in the world to explore and experiment and make mistakes, time goes by fast. Your mother and I work very hard, but we cannot afford to pay for you to go to college. So you have to buckle down and do your best and put yourself in the best possible position to get scholarships and whatever other assistance is out there. And getting distracted by these knucklehead boys is not what we want for you."

"But...."

"No buts," he said, waving his hand at her. "We have to be able to trust you to make the right decisions and since we can't, we have to make sure you don't get too far off track."

"I can't believe this," Nia said out loud.

"I know this is hard for you to understand right now but we are just trying to keep you safe and protect you," he continued. "Do you understand?"

"Yes," Nia said, sniffling.

"Good." He went to the stove and turned off the gumbo. "Do you want some?" he asked, pulling two bowls out of the cabinet.

"I'm not hungry," Nia said. She stood up and walked to the doorway. "I'm just going to go to bed."

"Okay," he said, ladling some of the stew into his bowl. "It'll be in the fridge if you change your mind."

But Nia was already up the stairs, tears running down her face.

***

That Monday, Nia still felt horrible. She hadn't been able to talk to Brandon — her parents also took her cell phone that weekend — so she didn't know how she was going to tell him what happened. Since Brandon had not heard from her all weekend, he figured Nia was grounded, but he was so anxious to know the details that he texted Patrice to get the scoop.

"Girl, your man is so worried about you that he's reaching out to me!" Patrice told Nia during their lunch break.

"Yeah, I'm phoneless right now," Nia said, looking dejected. Patrice's thumbs began working furiously on her phone, and then, in her typical dramatic fashion, she hit send.

"I told him your folks took your phone and to come meet you here after school so y'all can talk."

"Um, how exactly is that going to work, Patrice? He's got to get over here from Douglass, and don't forget I've got PJ to look after."

"Oh, I forgot about PJ. But Douglass is only about ten minutes away. I'll give you a ride home. Can't you just take the chance?"

"Really? I'm already grounded, phoneless, and boyfriend-less because I took a chance!" Nia practically yelled.

"Jeez! I'm sorry, girl. I was just trying to help y'all out." Patrice sent Brandon another text: *Never mind.* But it was too late. After receiving Patrice's first text, Brandon decided to skip his last class and head over to Mays High. He texted Patrice his location when he arrived so she and Nia could find him easily. After the final bell rang, there he was, waiting in the parking lot.

"Hey," he said, shoving his hands in his pockets. "How did it go?"

Nia took a deep breath. "Well, they found out. I'm grounded and they want us to take a break."

"Take a break?" Brandon looked confused.

"Yeah, I'm not supposed to talk to you for a while." She looked up at the sky and let out a loud sigh. "So yeah, that's how it went."

"I'm sorry, Nia," he said. "I didn't mean to get you in trouble."

"It's not your fault," Nia said. "I should have been more careful." She cleared her throat and looked Brandon in the eyes. "Well, I have to get home." She turned and took off toward Patrice without waiting for him to respond.

For practically that whole day, Nia had felt like there was a spotlight on her. Nobody had said anything to her, but she just had a feeling that something wasn't quite right. She'd noticed whispers and giggles when she had entered the classroom and wasn't sure if it was something about her or just her imagination.

She mentioned this to Patrice on the ride home. "Okay, what was going on today? Did it seem like everybody was acting weird to you?"

Patrice took a deep breath. While stopped at a red light, she pulled out her cell phone. "Somehow somebody started a rumor saying you and Brandon had sex at the movies this weekend," she said, showing Nia the messages on Instagram.

"Nikki tagged me. I tried to tell her it wasn't true, but she thought I was just saying that because you're my friend."

"What?" Nia couldn't believe this. Not only was she dealing with her parents' disappointment, but now she had to deal with fake gossip too?

"I know, girl." Patrice patted her arm. "But it'll blow over soon. Somebody else will do something, and people will forget about you. Just gotta make it through this week."

"But who started the rumor?" Nia was practically screeching now.

"It was probably Jackie, Mr. Ivey's daughter. She probably overheard him talking about it to your mom." When they got to Nia's driveway, Patrice leaned over and gave Nia a hug. "But you know it's not true. I know it's not true. Let people talk. It's not like you can stop them anyway."

Nia wiped unwelcome tears from her eyes. "I can't believe this."

"I'm sorry," Patrice said.

"I'll be fine," Nia said, shaking her head. "I gotta get inside and get settled before I go get PJ at his bus stop. I'll see you tomorrow."

Later that night, as Nia was lying in bed, she thought, *I'm not going to let this whole situation get me down.* She was feeling lucky that she had a good friend like Patrice.

Let's Talk

Where do we start?

First, let me say that as a doctor, I see young women in my office all the time that have boyfriends and, like Nia, aren't sure if they are ready to take that next step. Let me spend a minute here telling you what I've often told them.

Sex can be a wonderful experience shared between two people who care about each other. There's a reason why everyone talks about it. Our sexuality is part of what it means to be human.

It's also why I caution young patients to take their time. Sex in the moment can feel good and pleasurable but there are a slew of consequences that teens often aren't yet ready to handle.

We will talk about some of those physical consequences later in the book but for now, I want to have a heart-to-heart conversation with you about the emotional consequences.

As Nia quickly found out, it's not easy to navigate your sexuality as a teen. You might feel like you're ready to have sex but there are doubts in the back of your mind.

As my father used to tell me: "Doubt means don't." If there's any part of you that feels like you need more time or if you don't feel comfortable, don't do it. According to recent studies, only about half of high school students have ever had sex, and the average age when people start having sex is seventeen.

That means plenty of teens graduate high school without ever having sex. Despite what we see in the media and what our friends might say, there are plenty of people who wait until they are older to have sex. If you're the last one of your friends to lose your virginity, that's okay, especially when there's so much at stake. Here are a few things I want every young woman to know:

You are the Prize

There's a disturbing pattern that I see often in the young ladies I mentor and speak to at conferences. They believe that there is more power in being in a relationship—even a bad one—than being single and content with yourself.

While it is lovely to have a boyfriend who loves and respects you, there has to be a certain level of self-love that reminds you that you are worthy and valuable too. So, if your boyfriend is pressuring you to have sex and you're not ready, there's no shame in breaking up with him. Remember that you are the prize.

Sex and Love Are Not the Same Thing

There's more than one way to show someone you love or care for them. Sex isn't the only expression of love in a relationship, and it definitely isn't showing love if you have to be pressured into it.

No One Else Should Feel Entitled to Your Body

No matter who you are dating or what they believe, *you* are the only person who has a say in what you do with your body. Use that power wisely and make sure that any actions you take are because *you* want to take them. Other people can chime in, but you make the final decision, every time.

One more point I want to stress to young women is that you can change your mind at any time. Even if you have been kissing a boy and it feels like you two might be headed toward having sex, you can say—at any time—that you are no longer comfortable and would like to stop.

It is Very Easy to Get a Bad Reputation

As we saw with Nia, it is very easy for people to say whatever they want about you. Don't give them the ammunition. Even though Nia didn't have sex with Brandon, it was very easy for someone to spread the rumor that she had. This means that you have to be wise with your decisions and consider the consequences of behaving in ways that you don't want anyone else to know about.

There is a sexual double standard which means girls are judged more harshly than boys for what they do sexually. A boy has sex with a girl and he might be congratulated by his friends and family. If a girl has sex, she's called names and shamed. It's always been that way. It may not be fair, but this is the society that we live in. Your best bet is to play by the rules.

"But, Dr. Henry," you might be thinking, "I read through all of that, and I actually think I *am* ready for sex. So what now?" Keep reading. We're getting to that in the next chapter.

What You Should Know: Social Media for Teens

Nia faced a cold reality when she discovered that her classmates had been spreading rumors about her on social media.

I consider myself lucky that social media wasn't around to capture all my missteps when I was a teenager. But for teens like you, that time has come and gone. Now, social media is the primary way we communicate, for good and bad.

With several ways to keep up with your friends on social media every day, it can feel like you always need to be connected; after all, that's how you figure out what's going on with your friends and how they know what's going on with you. But remember that it's okay to log out. You may feel like you are out of the loop or you are missing out on what people are saying or doing, but that kind of obsession with other people isn't good for you.

One thing I want to mention is that social media tends to heighten your fear of missing out on something cool—don't worry too much about that. What you see on someone's Instagram isn't always what their real life looks like. That goes for celebrities you follow as well. They might look like they're having a great time at all the parties and hanging out with their friends, but remember that most people only choose to post the good stuff online and leave the bad stuff off entirely.

It can make you feel like you don't measure up, when in fact, you're just looking at someone else's best moments and none of their mistakes.

Now that we've covered some of the don'ts with social media, it's important to know that social media is a great tool – as long as you know how to use it effectively! It's definitely not going anywhere, so I'd rather you know how to use it to your advantage.

Every day, young people like you use social media (Instagram, Snapchat and others) to make money and pursue their passions before they're even out of high school. You can joke with your friends online and use it for homework, but don't sleep on how you can use social media to make a name for yourself before you even graduate from high school. Use these platforms to speak up about things you're passionate about or that you want to pursue when you're older. If you like beauty and makeup, why not review products on YouTube? If you're into art, why not share your art on Instagram? (Be sure to watermark it first!) If you're really good at math, like Nia, you can become a tutor and advertise your services online. The possibilities are endless.

Chapter Four: 2 Unwanted Gifts—Wish I Could Give Them Back!

"I can't believe you two finally had sex," Nia whispered to Patrice while in line at Chipotle. It was a month after the movie theater incident and Nia finally had her license. Her father had fixed up his old Toyota Corolla for her to drive. She celebrated by taking Patrice to get the hookup from Brandon's brother Mike. After so many years working there, he had moved his way up to manager and now they were able to get free burritos and drinks every so often. Nia wondered what Mike knew about her and Brandon, and she had to fight the urge to ask him how Brandon was doing. Instead, she just picked up her tray and sat down at one of the high tabletops by the window.

"So how was it? Did it hurt?"

"At first? Yeah," Patrice said. "We had to stop! I was like, 'Boy, I don't think this is going to fit!'" She took a sip of her Sprite. "I wish someone had told me that."

"Um, *I* told you that," Nia reminded her.

"You did?"

"Yes! I told you what Shonda told me!"

"I must not have been paying attention," Patrice said, laughing. "Because I could've used a heads-up."

"You think you'll do it again?" Nia asked.

"I don't know," Patrice admitted. "Felt like a whole lot of build-up and then it was over before it started."

"What do you mean?"

"It wasn't like in the movies," Patrice said, pausing to take a bite of her burrito. "It was just…I dunno, basic. Like, one, two, three, we were done."

"Does Marcus want to do it again?"

"Of course he does." She shook her head and smiled. "He's just happy he's not the only one of his friends who hasn't gotten any yet."

"He's probably the first," Nia said. "You know boys be lying."

"Girl, right!"

They ate in silence for a minute. "You and Brandon still on a break or whatever it is your parents call it?" Patrice asked.

"I don't know," Nia said. The truth was, she missed him but being together seemed to cause more trouble than it was worth. Her parents were still upset about what happened at the movie theater and every time she got in the car to go somewhere, they were calling and texting every five minutes to see where she was and who she was with.

She looked down at her phone and counted two phone calls (one from each parent) and three texts from her mom since they had pulled up. She took a quick minute to text her mom where she was and then turned her attention back to Patrice.

Patrice nodded. "I know you miss him."

"I do!" Nia replied, dreamily.

"Maybe you need to talk to your parents, then."

Nia smirked. "Is that what you did? You sat your parents down and told them you were going to have sex with Marcus?"

"Kind of," Patrice replied, and Nia almost choked on her chips.

"Wait, what?"

Patrice laughed at Nia's reaction. "I didn't tell you?"

"No!" Nia said, sipping her drink to get her cough under control. "What did you tell them?"

"Well," Patrice leaned back in her chair. "I told my mom that Marcus and I were in love and that we were thinking about…you know."

"And your mother didn't slap you into next week?"

"She didn't!" Patrice said. "She sat me down and talked my ear off, girl. I mean, like three hours of questions and *How do you know you love him* and *What does Marcus say* and *How long have you two been talking about this*."

"Wow."

"And then she took me to an appointment with her gynecologist. Her doctor put me on birth control at that first appointment."

"What are you on?"

"The pill. I'm thinking about switching to something else, though. I don't want to be bothered taking something every day when I'm not having sex every day, you know?"

"I can't believe it," Nia said. "I've known your mom forever and I would've bet she would have grounded you for life. But she was so cool about *everything*."

"Don't get it twisted, though," Patrice warned. "She doesn't want me having sex."

"But...?" Nia was confused.

"She said she just wants me to be safe, and she was telling me how sex changes everything. Like, *everything*. She told me she was my age when she started having sex and she regretted not waiting for someone better. She said she wished she had waited for my dad."

"Aww, that's cute."

"I think Marcus was worth it though," she said, sipping her drink. "At least I hope he is."

Patrice got quiet and Nia took that as an opportunity to satisfy her curiosity. "Okay, so I have more questions for you."

"Shoot."

"Did you bleed everywhere?"

"No." Patrice scrunched up her face. "It wasn't like I had my period. It was a little something afterward but not a lot."

"Did you guys do other stuff? Like...blowjobs?"

"No." Patrice shook her head. "I don't do that."

"I heard boys like it," Nia said, shrugging.

"Good for them, but that don't mean I have to do it," Patrice said, laughing.

"True. Did he...you know, on you?"

"Girl, if you are thinking about having sex you've got to be able to actually *say* what you're talking about," Patrice told her. "Why are you acting so shy?"

Nia blushed. "I'm just...awkward."

"You think you're going to lose your V-card anytime soon?"

"I don't know," Nia said. "Maybe. Brandon hasn't mentioned it yet."

"It's not about Brandon," Patrice reminded her. "What do *you* want?"

"I'm scared of getting pregnant," Nia admitted. "I don't want any kids any time soon." *PJ is enough of a handful,* she thought to herself.

"I feel you on that," Patrice said. "Wouldn't it be great if sex was just sex and you got pregnant by like, I dunno, going to the store and picking out a baby?"

"But then people wouldn't get any work done; they'd be too busy humping," Nia said, cracking up at her own joke.

"True, true." Patrice's voice turned serious all of a sudden.

"Maybe you should talk to your mom. She might be more understanding than you think."

"I don't know. I'm still thinking she might be the 'slap-me-into-next-week' type."

"You never know until you talk to her." Patrice scooped up the foil wrapper and napkins and tossed them into the trash. "I thought my mom would flip out too but she didn't."

Nia nodded thoughtfully. Something to consider at least. "Yeah, we'll see."

The two of them made their way to Nia's car. On the way to Patrice's house they blasted Bobby D's latest song and sang until their throats were hoarse.

When they pulled up in the driveway, Nia noticed Patrice's dad was home. He was a nice enough guy, but she was always a little uncomfortable around him. He was an officer with the Atlanta Police Department and seeing him around the house with his uniform on was a bit intimidating.

I wonder how he reacted to his daughter getting on birth control, Nia wondered.

They came in the front door and quickly made a beeline for the family room, where they could continue their conversation. "My cell phone's dead," Patrice said, glancing down at it. "Let me go plug it up."

She left for a few minutes and soon returned, bringing some chocolate cake with her. "You want some?" she offered, holding out the plate to Nia. Nia grabbed the small slice and ate it quickly.

"So, like I was saying," Patrice said, through a mouthful of cake, "you should talk to your mom. Or your dad."

"I think I will," Nia said. "I mean, what do I have to lose?"

Just then, Patrice's dad came into the family room, smiling wide at his daughter. "So you're the one who swiped my cake," he said. "I went to go get some and there was a big hunk missing!"

"My bad," Patrice said, finishing up the slice on her plate. "I didn't know it was yours."

"Sure you didn't," he said. He turned to Nia. "Hey, Nia. It's been a minute since you've been over here. How's your family doing?"

"They're good," Nia replied, trying to wipe any lingering crumbs off her face.

He nodded. "Good, good. I'll have to try to catch up with your dad. We're supposed to go to the Hawks game next week."

"Okay, I'll tell him to call you."

He saluted Nia, then headed back into the kitchen.

The girls kept talking for a few more minutes when they both heard a *ding* and a low grunt come from the other room.

"What is this?" Patrice's father walked back in the room, holding Patrice's cell phone high. "Who is this from?"

Even from across the room, Nia could see very clearly that Marcus had sent Patrice a photo where he wasn't wearing anything on his lower half.

Her dad gripped the cell phone and scowled at his daughter. "What is this?" he repeated.

Nia reached for her book bag on the floor and inched it closer to her feet, trying to gracefully figure out how to get out of the line of fire. Patrice shifted on the couch but didn't respond.

"Why is this boy—I'm assuming it's Marcus—sending you photos of his junk?" he asked, his face turning red.

"I'm going to get out of here," Nia whispered to both of them. She turned to Patrice. "I'll see you in school, tomorrow?" Patrice's father didn't move as Nia slipped past him quietly.

As she hit the front porch, Nia could still hear her friend's dad fussing about the photo.

She walked down the driveway and just said to herself quietly, "Thank God that it's not me this time."

***

Can you please come over?

Patrice's text message sounded urgent so Nia hopped in the car and drove the five miles to her best friend's house. She hadn't seen Patrice much in the past two weeks, since her father discovered Marcus' sext. Nia was shocked to realize Patrice still had her cell phone.

When she pulled up in the driveway she didn't see either of Patrice's parents' cars, so she felt a little more at ease. They'd be able to talk openly about whatever crisis Patrice found herself in.

When her friend opened the door, she looked as though she had been crying. Her brown skin looked dehydrated and puffy, and she had big dark circles underneath her eyes. Patrice, usually the most stylish person Nia knew, was dressed in mismatched pajamas and thick grey fuzzy socks. She waved Nia in and quickly shut the door behind her.

"Girl, what's going on?" Nia asked, trying to get a good look at her friend. Patrice was trembling. She looked like she was literally shaking with rage.

Patrice took a deep breath. "The other day when I woke up, I went to the bathroom and it hurt. Real bad. I thought it was a bladder infection — I used to get them when I was younger — so I didn't think anything of it."

"Did you go to the doctor?"

Patrice sat on the couch with her head in her hands and nodded. "Yeah, I went Friday. Just got the results a couple hours ago. Chlamydia and gonorrhea. *Two* STDs? I feel so dirty. I can't believe he would do this to me!"

Nia sat down and rubbed her friend's shoulders. "Dang, girl, I'm so sorry. Did they give you the medicine for it already?"

Patrice dug around in her purse for the little paper bag filled with her medications. "I just have to take these and then I should be okay. I'm just glad I went, because who knows how long I could have been walking around with it, you know?"

"Did y'all use a condom?" Nia asked softly, trying not to blame her friend, but wanting to know if she at least tried to protect herself.

"Well, no!" Patrice said, her eyes watering. "I mean, Marcus told me he wasn't with anybody else before me which is why I'm totally shocked. I didn't expect *this*."

"Did you tell your mom? Have you told Marcus?"

"Yes and yes. My mom went with me. I texted him right away. He's acting like he had no idea."

Nia was silent for a moment. She liked Marcus and didn't think he was the type of guy to knowingly spread STDs. But this incident made her think maybe she didn't know Marcus that well.

"Do you believe him?"

"No," Patrice said flatly. "And I don't care what he says. I'm smarter than this. I can't be with a guy who gives me a disease, whether he knew about it or not."

Nia just nodded and waited for her friend to say something else.

Patrice leaned back on the couch and let out a long, deep sigh. "This is horrible. My mom is too through with me right now. She trusted me, and look what happened. This sucks so much, but at least I'm not pregnant."

"Yeah, that's good." Nia looked around the living room for some source of inspiration, something she could tell her friend to make her feel better. But she came up empty. So she just decided to just say what was in her heart. "I'm sorry this happened to you. I know how much you liked Marcus."

One lone tear streaked down Patrice's cheek. "I really did love him," she said softly. "But now that's over. You can bet I won't be chasing behind any boys any time soon."

Nia leaned over to hug Patrice and let her cry softly on her shoulder.

Let's Talk

Perhaps you, like Nia and Patrice, think you are ready to have sex. Your boyfriend is ready, you are curious about what it feels like, and you're convinced you're ready to take your relationship to the next level.

I always tell my teenage patients that sex is an adult activity, primarily because adults are best equipped to handle the consequences that can arise from sex. But, if you're thinking you're ready, I'd like to walk you through the set of questions I ask my patients to help them make the most informed decision.

Do I know how to protect myself from unintended pregnancy and Sexually Transmitted Diseases (STDs)?

This is the first question I ask teens because there is a lot of misinformation out there on how girls get pregnant and how STDs get transmitted. These myths have been around for decades, but now it's easier than ever to get accurate information thanks to technology.

In the next chapter, I will break down all these myths and share the truth about STD and pregnancy prevention.

Would having a child right now delay or hinder my educational pursuits?

In most cases, the answer is yes. Even for adults, having a child is a life-changing experience.

Once you become a parent, you must forever factor in what's best for your child—and it doesn't always match what's best or easiest for you. That's why I talk to my teen patients about waiting, because this is the time in your life that you can be completely selfish. I want you to enjoy this freedom of being a teenager because once it's gone, it's gone forever.

Of course, it's entirely possible to have a child and get a degree at the same time. You may even have friends or family members who've done it. But if you ask them about it, I'll bet they will probably tell you that it was hard work and came with a lot of sleepless nights and worries about whether they could do it. Having a child while you're still in school means your attention will be split between schoolwork and child care, no matter how involved the father is.

Do I have a healthy relationship with my partner?

Before you lay down with someone, it is important that the foundation of your relationship is strong. Most teens are new to relationships. You might be modeling what you've seen in your parents' lives or on TV, but you really aren't sure how *you* would define a good relationship. Here are a few things I encourage young women to consider about their boyfriends before they decide to have sex:

- *Is he kind to me? Has anyone expressed concern for the way he treats me?*
- *When I talk about my concerns, does he listen?*
- *Is he quick to get angry if I say or do something he doesn't like?*
- *Does my boyfriend trust me? Do I trust him?*
- *Does he criticize me or make negative comments about girls in general?*
- *Is he honest with me?*
- *Is our relationship fair (i.e., we don't just do what he wants to all the time)?*

You have to answer these questions honestly. Being in love (or even just "like") with a guy can sometimes cloud your judgment, but feelings aren't facts. It is your job to protect yourself at all times.

Am I comfortable discussing sex with my partner?

This is a big question because sex is as much verbal as it is physical. For anyone, teens or adults, sex should always begin with a conversation. You need to be on the same page as far as how you two plan to protect yourselves from pregnancy and STDs and whether you two know what sex would mean for your relationship. Some girls may think that having sex will deepen their bond, and maybe the guy is just thinking it's a fun way to spend an afternoon. Before you get intimate, be sure you are in agreement with what sex will mean. If you're not comfortable having these sorts of conversations, I'm willing to bet you aren't ready to take that next step.

Am I comfortable discussing sex with my parents?

Even with perfect usage, birth control sometimes fails or you may need to see a doctor about a possible STD. When these issues occur, it's likely you will need to let your parents know.

Some teen patients will try to ask me not to tell their parents (and if they are over 18, I do not legally have to tell their parents anything, even if they ask me). But if you are on your parents' insurance, they will find out when they get the bill for the visit.

This is why I always encourage teens to be open and honest with their parents. They've been teenagers before. They know what it's like and it's better to have them on your team than to keep them in the dark. The more trusted adults in your corner, the better.

This is why it's also important for you to be open and honest with your doctor.

If you were to experience any physical symptoms of an STD or think you might be pregnant, it's good to be upfront about that when you see the doctor. Trust me—we've seen it all and we won't judge you. But if you try to hide information from your doctor, it makes it that much harder to get any treatment you may need. Plus, if we have the whole story, it makes it easier for us to help you have a conversation with your parents about what's going on.

Let's Talk About Sexting

Did you know that sexting is illegal in most states if you are a teenager? The law considers the possession of any sexually explicit photo (whether it's of you or someone else) of someone under the age of eighteen to be child pornography. The penalties vary but this is not a charge you want to go on your record.

The main thing to keep in mind is that those images are out there permanently. With all the technology that exists, you may think that because you deleted an image or video that it's gone, but it's not. It may be gone from your phone, but it could exist on the cloud as well.

Once you take a nude or semi-nude photo or video of yourself and send it to a boyfriend or girlfriend, that's it. You no longer have control over that image. That person can send it to all of their friends and soon everyone knows what you look like naked. Even if you trust the person you sent it to, they could lose the phone and then your photos are out there for the world to see. Someone can take your image and manipulate it or have your name associated with a website you wouldn't want to find yourself on.

The easiest way to handle it is to avoid taking any sexually explicit photos of yourself and let your friends know you don't want their photos either. Chances are your friends don't know that it's illegal. Simply tell them, "You know you might go to jail for that, right?"

Let's Talk - The 7 STDs Everyone Should Know About

The best thing you can do is to arm yourself with knowledge. The information I'm sharing in this section is crucial to your physical and mental well-being. In my presentations, I talk about STDs and their symptoms. I'm a doctor; people expect me to talk about the medical side of things. But I also talk about the emotional realities—how an unplanned pregnancy or positive STD test can be devastating to a teen.

If you think you are ready to have sex, read this section first. It's not meant to scare you but to inform you of the risks of being sexually active.

STDs are more common than most teens realize. Nearly 40% of teen girls between 14 and 19 will contract an STD.

That means that if you think about ten of your sexually active friends, at least four of them will have to go to the doctor to get treatment for a sexually transmitted disease. I don't like those odds, which is why I want to be sure every teen girl I see understands the risks and how to best protect herself.

You can't tell who has an STD by just looking at them. (You can't even tell if they're naked!) Many STDs don't have any symptoms or those symptoms might not be active at the time you're with that person. The only way to be sure someone doesn't have an STD is to get tested and share the results with each other.

As I mentioned in a previous chapter, if you're not able to discuss how you are going to protect yourself, you're not ready to have sex. It may feel like an awkward conversation, but it can be a lifesaving one. So if you don't feel like you can ask your partner if they've been tested and insist on using contraception to protect yourself, it is best that you remain abstinent until you can. Some guys might not have ever asked their doctor to test them for STDs and might be offended at the suggestion that they should get tested before being intimate with you. The reality is that STDs do not discriminate. You can contract one (or more) of them the first time you have sex.

It doesn't matter if you are a good student or if you come from a rich family. That's why it's important to be diligent and protect yourself. You only get one body, so keep it as healthy as you can.

A quick note: In these descriptions of STDs, you'll notice I use terms like "sexual activity" versus simply "sex." Lots of young people are always looking for loopholes in sex. Some try to lessen their risk of pregnancy or disease by doing everything *but* penetration, such as having oral sex. Any time you come in contact with someone's bodily fluids (blood, semen or vaginal secretions) there is a risk associated with it. I use the term "sexual activity" to remind you that even if you are one of those "everything but" teens, you still need to protect yourself.

Chlamydia

Chlamydia is one of the most common sexually transmitted diseases. It is a tricky disease because up to 70% of the people who have it show no symptoms. This means that most people who contract chlamydia don't realize it until a doctor tests them. If you feel fine—not experiencing anything out of the ordinary—you might not suspect you have anything to worry about. There are over a million new cases reported each year, most common among women. It's transmitted through oral, vaginal or anal sexual contact with someone carrying the disease.

Symptoms

For those women who do experience symptoms, they will usually have vaginal discharge and frequent, painful urination.

Complications

If untreated, chlamydia can cause infertility, which means when you do decide you are ready to have children, you may have a harder time doing so. The reason for this is that chlamydia can lead to pelvic inflammatory disease (PID), which causes scarring and blocking of your fallopian tubes.

Diagnosis & Treatment

If your doctor suspects chlamydia, she will either do a cervical swab, which tests the cellular material collected from the cervix during a pap smear, or collect a urine sample. It will take about five to seven days to get the results back and then antibiotics will be prescribed to clear up the infection.

After receiving treatment you will need to be retested within three months.

HPV

Another one of those "invisible" infections is the human papillomavirus or HPV. It is the number one sexually transmitted disease, with nearly 25% of the population carrying it. The CDC estimates that there are 14 million new cases every year—and the majority does not know they have it! HPV is so common that nearly all sexually active people contract it at some point in their lives.

Symptoms

Like chlamydia, most of the time it shows no symptoms. However, some types of HPV can cause genital warts, which may look like a smooth, flesh-colored bump or a group of bumps that look a bit like cauliflower.

These are generally painless, but some people do experience itching. HPV is transmitted through oral, vaginal or anal sexual (or simply skin-to-skin) contact with someone carrying the disease.

Complications

There are several strains of HPV that cause cancer. In 2006, the HPV vaccine Gardasil hit the market. Designed for girls and for boys ages 9-26, it is a three dose series, completed over six months. It offers protection against the four virus strains that cause the majority of cervical cancers, anal cancers, and genital warts. The Gardasil-9 targets five additional strains. The side effects of the shots are pain, swelling, redness, bruising, itching, lump at the shot site, headache, fever and dizziness. The most serious side effects are fainting and blood clots. It does offer protection even in patients already infected with HPV, however the goal is vaccination before the patient is ever exposed to it. It's not possible to "catch" HPV from the vaccination.

Diagnosis & Treatment

There aren't any blood, urine or oral swab tests available for HPV (and none at all for men) so women should get tested for the virus during their routine Pap smears. If genital warts are present, there are a few methods doctors can use to remove them. One is something called cryotherapy, where the warts are frozen with liquid nitrogen every 1-2 weeks until they are all removed. Other options include topical solutions containing acid to chemically burn the warts or removing them surgically.

Gonorrhea

Gonorrhea is the second most common sexually transmitted bacterial infection, behind chlamydia. Almost a half a million people were diagnosed with gonorrhea in 2016. Since there are generally no symptoms, the number of people with gonorrhea might actually be significantly higher. Gonorrhea and chlamydia often travel together in pairs, so doctors often test for them together. Like chlamydia, gonorrhea is a bacteria that can cause long-term damage if left untreated. It is transmitted through oral, vaginal or anal sexual contact with someone carrying the disease.

Symptoms

Gonorrhea can cause painful urination, vaginal discharge or bleeding between periods. It can also occur as rectal itching, soreness and bleeding or painful bowel movements, particularly in those who have had anal sex. If you've engaged in unprotected oral sex, it can cause a sore throat.

But often gonorrhea appears with no symptoms. This is why getting tested regularly is so crucial.

Complications

Again, like chlamydia, untreated gonorrhea can cause pelvic inflammatory disease, which can lead to infertility and pelvic pain.

Diagnosis & Treatment

If a doctor suspects gonorrhea, she will do either a cervical swab or a urine test. It will take about a week to get the results back and then antibiotics will be prescribed to clear up the infection. You should be retested within three months.

Herpes

If you've been paying attention thus far, you'll begin to notice that all these diseases are fairly common. Herpes is no different. There are two strains of herpes: type 1 and type 2. Type 1 is more common in the mouth and type 2 is more common in the genitals, but either type can be present in either area. An estimated 50%-90% of adults have oral herpes by age 50 and up to 25% of adults have genital herpes. The CDC estimates that there are over 750,000 new herpes infections each year in the U.S. The virus is transmitted by contact with an infected area (genitals or otherwise) or through contact with secretions (saliva, vaginal secretions or semen) infected with the virus. It's important to note that type 1 can potentially infect someone genitally by performing oral sex on them; and vice-versa; someone with genital type 2 can infect someone who performs oral sex on them.

Symptoms

Herpes, unfortunately, is an STD with no cure. People who have herpes can develop painful, red blisters on their mouth or genitals. Some can even feel the tingling and burning before the blisters actually develop. An outbreak can last anywhere from a week to a month. During the initial outbreak, patients might also have a headache, sore throat and other flu-like symptoms.

Complications

Having herpes increases the risk of contracting HIV (more on HIV in a few sections). Also, because there is no cure, herpes requires long-term care and monitoring. It is a disease you have to learn to live with and that includes taking precautions with *every single person* you sleep with moving forward.

Diagnosis & Treatment

If a doctor suspects a possible herpes outbreak, they will either order a blood test or swab the lesion on the skin. It usually takes a week to receive the results. Treatment for the disease focuses mainly on the outbreaks to try to minimize their frequency and severity. Patients will take antiviral medication for 7-10 days for initial outbreak and then for 2-5 days for any outbreaks after that. Some people get herpes outbreaks so often that they must take antiviral medication daily.

Syphilis

Syphilis is one of the least common STDs, but I still caution teens about its prevalence because of its damaging long-term effects. It is a bacterial STD that occurs in three stages. The first, or primary, stage is when most people develop a chancre, which is a painless, firm and round sore.

It will last anywhere from three to six weeks and will often heal without treatment, however, that doesn't mean you don't need to see your doctor. Without treatment, syphilis will progress to the secondary stage where rashes will appear on one or more areas of the body.

It will look like rough, red or reddish brown spots on the palms of the hands or soles of the feet. People with syphilis may also have large white or gray lesions on their underarms, mouth and groin. For those who go untreated, syphilis will reach the third stage, where the damage goes deeper. The bacteria attack the internal organs such as the brain, eyes and heart.

Symptoms

Besides the skin lesions and rashes mentioned earlier, people may experience hair loss, headaches, swollen lymph nodes, fever, weight loss, muscle aches and fatigue.

Complications

If left untreated, syphilis can cause blindness, dementia, paralysis, numbness and muscle movement disorders.

Diagnosis & Treatment

If your doctor suspects a possible syphilis infection, she will order a blood test. Syphilis is curable but if treatment was delayed, the medicine will not repair the damage that was already done. Antibiotics will clear up a syphilis infection over the course of at least a month.

Hepatitis

There are three types of hepatitis: A, B and C. Hepatitis A is generally spread by ingesting food or water that is contaminated by microscopic amounts of feces or from one person to another by fecal-oral contact. By fecal-oral contact, I am specifically referring to the sexual practice known as "rimming" or "eating booty." This type of activity can potentially be a source of Hepatitis A infection when sexually active with an infected partner. Hepatitis B and C are transmitted through contact with bodily fluids (including blood) of an infected person. As with the other diseases already discussed, all forms of sexual activity with someone infected with either Hepatitis B or C put you at risk. According to the CDC, there were an estimated 2200 acute Hepatitis A infections, 19,200 acute Hepatitis B infections, and 30,500 acute Hepatitis C infections in 2014.

Symptoms

All forms of hepatitis can cause the same types of symptoms: fever, fatigue, nausea, vomiting, abdominal pain, jaundice, appetite loss and gray looking bowel movements.

Complications

Chronic Hepatitis B and C may progress to cirrhosis (a liver disease) or liver cancer.

Diagnosis & Treatment

If your doctor suspects hepatitis, he or she will order a blood test.

Hepatitis A will clear up on its own, as will an acute* hepatitis B infection. However, for a chronic** hepatitis B & C infection (one lasting more than six months) the doctor will prescribe antiviral medication. In addition, there are vaccines available for prevention of Hepatitis A and B.

*An acute infection lasts from a few days to several weeks.
**A chronic infection lasts three months or longer.

HIV/AIDS

I saved this one until the end because I find that HIV is the one STD my patients are most afraid of. Human immunodeficiency virus (HIV) is another one of those "invisible" diseases. Many people who have HIV have no outward signs of the disease and have very few symptoms in the initial stages. HIV has been a public health crisis since the 1980s (before most of you reading this were born!) and while the treatments have improved each year, the number of people contracting the virus has remained high. More than 1.2 million Americans have been diagnosed with HIV or AIDS (Acquired Immune Deficiency Syndrome).

It's important to note that you cannot catch the virus from doing mundane, everyday things like shaking someone's hand or being in the same room when a person with HIV coughs. You cannot catch HIV from a toilet seat or from sharing a glass. It is not transmitted through sweat, saliva or tears. HIV is transmitted through vaginal, anal and oral sexual activity (although oral is less likely). It can also be transmitted through drug use or from mother to child during childbirth or breastfeeding.

Symptoms

People with HIV can show no symptoms for years after they've been infected. The many common symptoms are weight loss, fatigue, fever, muscle ache or a skin rash, which are common, non-specific symptoms for many diseases.

Complications

By its very definition, HIV is a disease that weakens your immune system. This means it's easier for you to develop secondary infections that are much harder for your body to fight.

Diagnosis & Treatment

The only way to know you have HIV is to get tested. Your doctor will order a blood test and you will get the results back within a week, just like with the other STD tests. As scary as it may be to hear your doctor say she wants to test you for HIV, it is far better to know your status than to be unsure about what's happening in your body.

Prevention

There are a few things you can do to decrease your risk of catching any of the seven STDs I've outlined: choose abstinence, practice mutual monogamy and use condoms and dental dams correctly and consistently. I go over more about each of these in the section below.

Abstinence

I'll say it again: If you are not comfortable having conversations about STDs and pregnancy with someone you're interested in having sex with, then you shouldn't be having sex. Abstinence is a great choice for those who would rather not deal with any of these potential consequences. It will give you peace of mind and you can focus on other things—your schoolwork, friendships and other interests.

Mutual Monogamy

"Mutual" monogamy is the key word here. If you or any of your friends are considering being sexually active, then you need to understand that you can take all the precautions to protect yourself, but if your partner isn't *also* doing those things, you are still at risk. That means if you want to have sex with someone and they are also having sex with other people, your risk of contracting an STD increases.

Protection

All it takes is one act of unprotected sex to change the course of your life forever. Condoms and dental dams (thin pieces of latex that cover the vulva during oral sex) should be used *every* time you have sex, to protect you from both STDs and unplanned pregnancy.

It's important to note that with these diseases, using condoms only *decreases* your risk of contracting the disease. Even with proper use every time, there is no guarantee that the disease would not be passed to you, as most are transmitted through bodily fluids and, well, that's a big part of sex!

Another reason why STDs are so rampant is that it can be embarrassing to discover that you have one. People may look at you differently or assume something negative about your sex life. As a result, many people who get them are hesitant to tell their sexual partners, which means their partners don't get tested, or they end up just passing the infection back and forth. When they break up, those untreated sexual partners then go on to have sex with someone else and the STD continues to spread.

Be smart. Protect yourself at all times. Your number one priority should be your health. You can find another boyfriend, but your body is the only one you'll get. Treat it well.

What You Should Know – Sex Myths

There are so many myths about sex floating around that it can be hard to know what to believe. Can you get pregnant the first time you have sex? Is oral sex safer than other types of sex? Is it safe to just "pull out" rather than use a condom?

Knowledge is power, so let's talk about some of these myths. Take a few minutes to take the quiz below and I'll meet you in the answer key.

Sex Myths Quiz – Can you answer these true or false questions?

1. You can't get pregnant if you pee after sex. T F
2. You can't get pregnant if you have sex standing up. T F
3. Using two condoms decreases the chance of getting pregnant. T F
4. The pull-out method is a great, free form of birth control. T F
5. You can get pregnant the first time you have sex. T F
6. You shouldn't use a condom more than once. T F
7. You don't have to use protection for oral sex. T F
8. You can tell if someone has an STD by just looking at them. T F
9. It is safe to use an expired condom. T F

Answer Key:

1. **False.** While it is helpful to go to the bathroom after sex to help avoid urinary tract infections, using the bathroom isn't going to stop the sperm from carrying out their mission.
   They're strong little swimmers.
2. **False.** It doesn't matter what position you use. If sperm gets into the vagina, there's a chance you could make a baby. Again, sperm are strong swimmers. Gravity is not an effective form of birth control.
3. **Entirely false.** This myth has been around for a long time (I remember hearing it when I was a teen!) but it's actually dangerous advice.
   Using two condoms will actually *increase* the chance that you'll get pregnant because they will rub against each other, making breakage more likely. One condom is all you need. If you hear someone try to tell you otherwise, run in the other direction!
4. **False.** The trouble with "pulling out" (or as your doctor would call it, the withdrawal method) is twofold: one, most teen boys

cannot control their ejaculation to the point of making this effective and two, even pre-cum (what the penis secretes before ejaculation) contains enough sperm for a girl to get pregnant. It's popular because it doesn't require a trip to the doctor and it's cheap.
But it also has one of the highest failure rates of birth control. (For every 100 couples, 22 will get pregnant within a year using this method. That's a lot of babies!)

5. **True.** Sperm don't know it's your first time having sex. All they know is that they want to complete the mission—to find and fertilize an egg. Whether it's your first or 50th time having sex, it's possible to get pregnant. As long as a sperm and an egg are together, pregnancy is always possible.
6. **True.** Think of it this way — a condom is a barrier between you and someone else's bodily fluids. It's thin and fragile, particularly after it's been used. The condom may have tiny tears in it that you may not be able to see, meaning that it would allow the same infections it protected against the first time to pass through to you the second time it's used. Each sexual encounter requires a new condom.
7. **False.** A popular myth is that oral sex is "safer" than penetration. You may not have to worry about pregnancy with this act, but that doesn't mean it's risk free. Oral sex has the same risks as other types of sex. Any time you transfer bodily fluids (whether it's mouth to genitals or genitals to genitals) you risk contracting a sexually transmitted disease. For safer oral sex, you can use something called a dental dam. As a society we don't talk much about them, but they are thin pieces of latex that can be spread over the vulva to protect against disease during oral sex.
8. **False.** I hear this a lot from the patients in my office — those of all ages. But as we covered in the earlier sections, most STDs don't cause any symptoms. People can look perfectly healthy, but can still be infected with STDs. You can't look at someone and determine whether they are healthy.
9. **False.** Condoms have expiration dates for a reason. Over time, the latex gets dry and brittle, making it more likely to break.

Chapter Five: 1 Big Talk, Big Breath Taken and Fingers Crossed

By the time Nia made it home, she was exhausted. She dragged herself into the living room and plopped onto the couch. Her mom came in sorting the mail. She tossed some college brochures in her daughter's lap. "These came for you; these are some good schools. Make sure you check them out."

"I will." Nia put the brochures on the side table next to the couch and sat up straight. Her mom kept flitting around the room, straightening pillows, grabbing stray papers off the couch. Nia watched her mom for a minute, and then cleared her throat.

"Hey, Mom?"

"Yes, honey?"

"Can I talk to you for a minute?"

Her mom stopped and turned toward her daughter. "Of course. What's up?"

"Can you sit down?"

"Oh, this sounds serious," her mom said, making her way to the couch next to Nia. "Is something wrong?"

"No," Nia said, carefully. "I just have...some stuff I want to talk to you about. I feel like we haven't really talked since....everything happened with Brandon and I have...questions."

"Ah," her mom said. "Okay. Well, I always say that I want you to come to me with questions so...let me hear it."

Nia took a deep breath and began talking. Nia was nervous. She wasn't sure what her mom was going to say, but she was glad that she was at least willing to listen.

"Well," Nia began, "I was talking with some of my friends and they're all starting to have sex. I feel like I'm the only virgin out of everybody."

Her mom inhaled a bit and then tried to relax. "Okay. And how does that make you feel?"

"I mean, I know sex is supposed to be this big deal but it doesn't seem like anybody waits until marriage anymore. It makes me feel lame."

"I can understand that," her mom said. She leaned over to the side of the couch and picked up the photo album that was on the bottom shelf of the side table. She opened the album and smoothed out the wrinkled plastic covering. "Have I ever told you how I met your father?"

Nia shook her head.

"You and Brandon actually remind me of your dad and me," she said, flipping the page to show Nia a photo that looked like it was from the eighties, way back in the day. "We met in high school, you know."

"You did?"

She nodded. "Yup. And I was crazy about him. Ask your grandma sometime. We didn't have cell phones in those days, so I spent all my free time on the house phone with him, and your grandma would be fussing at me to stop tying up the line."

"Couldn't you just take the phone into your room?"

"Ha! You are so young. No. There was one phone and it was in the kitchen. If I wanted to have a conversation, that's where I had to stay." She flipped a few more pages and showed Nia a photo of her parents, dressed up in matching blue and white outfits.

"Is this from prom?"

"It is. You see how his tie matched my dress? Your daddy came up with that. I didn't care too much about what I wore. I just wanted to be sure he was *my* date." She studied the picture closely. "If I remember correctly, there was some other heffa that wanted him to go with her. But you see I won out, don't you?"

"Yeah, I see that. So you guys got together your senior year?"

"We did. Back then, it was so simple. We were just…in love. So I know how you feel right now. You're happy, this boy has you smiling all the time and your hormones are crazy. Yes, I remember that time very well."

"So did you and dad wait until college to have sex?"

Her mom nodded. "We did. I wanted to be sure he was worth it. You only get one first time so I wanted it to be with the right person. By that time, we had been together for a long time and he had proved himself trustworthy."

Nia felt a little uncomfortable, but she felt like this was the perfect time to ask the question that was on her mind. "So what was the first time like?"

Her mom looked up at the ceiling thoughtfully. "Well, it's been a while, but I remember it hurt like heck. But it was your father's first time too. So we didn't rush anything."

"Did you regret it, you know, because you and dad got divorced?"

"Your dad is a great man, Nia," her mom said. "We just weren't always great together. I don't regret being with him because then I wouldn't have you and PJ."

"But my whole life you've told me about how you had to drop out of school to have me," Nia reminded her. "You *just* got your degree and I'm sixteen years old. Doesn't that make you wish you had me later?"

Her mom closed the photo album and scooted closer to Nia. "Listen," she said carefully, "you are my world. If I didn't have you and PJ, yes, I would have been done with school a lot faster. But I don't regret having you. If anything, you've pushed me to grow up and to get my head together. I owe you a lot. Your father too."

Nia nodded while her mother continued. "But that doesn't mean that I want you to follow in my footsteps. I want you to have opportunities that I didn't. That's what every mom wants for her kids; for them to go further than she did. So even though I know you might feel like you are left out with your friends, know that you aren't missing out on anything that won't be perfect and special when it's the right time for you."

"How do I know when it's the right time?"

"You know what I've always wanted to tell you, but had to wait until you grew up a bit?" Her mom laughed a little, which made Nia raise an eyebrow as to what was coming next. "Sex is no fun when you've got to sneak and hide to do it. Like when you're scared a roommate or a parent might walk in on you because you're not living on your own yet. Sex is best when you are in a committed relationship, fully able to handle any of the consequences of sex on your own. That's what I want you to wait for."

"Wow," Nia said. "I didn't expect you to be so..."

"Honest?"

"No, not at all," Nia admitted. "I was thinking you were going to yell at me."

"I'm glad you came to me," her mom said. "I want you to feel safe asking me anything. I can't do that if I'm fussing at you."

She turned her body so she could face Nia directly. "So…does this conversation mean that you are thinking about having sex with Brandon?"

Nia's face turned red. "Um, I…I'm not sure."

"Well, I know once all your friends start having sex, you start wondering if you should too.

And that's normal, at your age. Thinking about sex and what it would be like is a part of growing up."

Nia just nodded and waited for her mother to continue. "I do think it would be best if you were to wait. Like I said earlier, sex can be so very special and I've got to tell you, kid—most of your friends who *are* having sex aren't having great sex."

"How do you know?" Nia asked, raising her eyebrow.

Her mom chuckled a little. "Because they're young and inexperienced. Sex is just an activity to them, like playing Madden. They haven't yet learned the secret to sex—that it's about real connection to another person."

"Most of the girls I've talked to said it wasn't that great," Nia admitted, thinking back to her conversation with Patrice earlier.

"Trust me, I know what I'm talking about. Once you get a little older, learn more about yourself and your body, what you like and dislike, sex will be great. But now? I don't think it's worth the trouble."

She shook her head. "There are so many risks involved. Is it really worth possibly exposing yourself to a disease—which you may or may not be able to get rid of—or possibly getting pregnant for a few minutes of sex that may not even feel good?"

Nia chewed on her lip and let her mother's words sink in.

"Trust me, I see this all the time at work," her mom said. "You know how many young girls come in needing a pregnancy test and antibiotics for an infection? These are the consequences you need to be prepared to face. Do you think you're ready for that?"

"God, no," Nia said, shaking her head.

"I'm suggesting you wait to have sex," her mom said slowly. "But I know ultimately it's your decision. That's why I want you to really think this through. Because I can have my reasons for telling you to wait, but *you* have to be sure of what you want to do."

She reached over and gave Nia a hug. "I love you more than anything. You know you're my favorite girl. If you have any other questions, you be sure to come talk to me, okay?"

"Okay," Nia said. "I will."

Let's Talk

I'm proud of Nia.

Even though it was uncomfortable to sit down with her mom and have a discussion about sex, she did it and her relationship with her mom is better for it. Even Patrice, who wound up getting more than she bargained for, was better off for having talked to her mother.

The reason why I'm speaking out in the community, talking to parents and teens, is to help get the ball rolling on being able to have conversations about sex. Like Nia's mom, I've seen what happens when no one talks about sex—teens are uninformed or misinformed, someone gets pregnant or contracts a disease and the parents are surprised by everything.

I get that talking to your parents about sex can be awkward. That's why most teens try to skip the talk and go right into having sex without their parents' knowledge. In my experience, that doesn't work out so well. Studies have shown that teens who have open conversations with their parents about safe sex are less likely to have an unintended pregnancy or be diagnosed with an STD.

A large majority of teens are embarrassed to talk to their parents about sex or feel like asking questions might cause their parents to make assumptions about their sex lives.

I'll be honest with you: Not every parent is ready to think about their child as a sexual being.

But ready or not, here you are.

I encourage parents that I speak with to be open-minded and actually listen to what their child is asking.

I've worked with teens to help them have these conversations with their parents and here are a few of my best tips on how to get the information you need without feeling embarrassed or ashamed:

What You Should Know—Conversation Starters

Timing is everything

Most parents will tell you that you can come to them with any question, any time. But we all know there are certain times that are better than others when it comes to having serious conversations about sex. Avoid trying to have a sit-down conversation when a parent is stressed about some bad news or is otherwise mentally preoccupied. Give them a minute to let those feelings subside.

Acknowledge how you feel

If you're a little embarrassed or unsure, tell your parents! Simply saying, "Mom, I'd like to ask you something, but I'm a little embarrassed about it" or "Dad, I'd like to talk to you about something but I'm scared of how you will react" can let them know that you need reassurance. It will help them understand where you are coming from, and give them a place to start the conversation.

A few conversation starters

- *"I heard someone say..."*
- *"What was dating like when you were my age?"*
- *"Our sex-ed teacher told us about...Is that true?*
- *"Some of the kids at school are..."*

If you are convinced that your parents won't be open to having these kinds of conversations, try to talk to another trusted adult (like an aunt or uncle) or a doctor about what you're considering.

Chapter Six: 3 Different Ways

Two Years Later

Nia looked around the crowded high school gym and took a deep breath. She always felt so small and invisible at college fairs, with people bustling everywhere and everyone seeming to be deep in conversation already. It was hard for her to walk up to people and just start talking, so she gave herself a challenge: she decided she'd stop at three tables and then she'd go home.

She stopped first at the University of Georgia table, glancing nervously at the brochures spread out on it. A middle-aged white woman behind the table smiled at Nia and started talking. "How are you today?"

"I'm…overwhelmed," Nia said, laughing. "There are so many people here."

The woman, whose name badge read "Susan," looked around the gym. "Yes, they had a great turnout this year. Some years, not so much." She handed Nia one of the brochures. "So, do you have any questions about UGA?"

"I know UGA is a pretty big school," Nia said carefully, unfolding the brochure to see big, smiling faces beaming back up at her. "How big are the classes usually?"

Susan clasped her hands in front of her. "Well, we do have larger classes, but we also have the First-Year Odyssey program, which connects incoming freshmen with faculty in a small class environment. There are generally less than 20 students in those, so you'll get that individual attention if that's what you're looking for."

They talked for a few more minutes, with Susan wishing Nia well and encouraging her to apply. Nia hit the Oglethorpe University table and made pleasant enough small talk with the representative there.

For her last stop, Nia walked up to a woman in a blue polo shirt staffing the table at Spelman College. "Hi, I'm Mya," she said happily, standing up and stretching out her hand for a handshake. "What's your name?"

"I'm Nia," she said, shifting her books to one side so she could reach out to shake Mya's hand with the other.

"So are you a senior?" Mya asked, her smile revealing two deep dimples. To Nia, it felt almost like looking in a mirror, as Mya had the same thick curly brown hair and cocoa-colored skin. If nothing else, the two of them could pass for sisters.

"Yes," Nia said. "I've got a few schools I'm applying to, but my parents really want me to look at a few more. They're anxious."

Mya laughed. "Yes, I remember when my parents were driving me crazy about college admissions too. But you'll make it through. Are you thinking about applying to Spelman?"

Nia nodded. "Yes, I took a tour last year and really liked the campus."

"The entire south side of campus is practically brand-new," Mya said. "I've only been there for a little over a year, but already it looks so different from when I toured as a senior."

"Oh, so you're a sophomore?"

"Yup. Graduated from Mays."

"I go to Mays!" Nia said, excited.

"You might know my brother, Caleb? He's a senior there now."

"Caleb's in my chemistry class," Nia said. "He's really smart."

Mya looked like a proud mama at the compliment. "Thank you. I taught him everything he knows."

"So you like Spelman?" Nia turned her attention to some of the brochures on the table. She spotted a financial aid pamphlet and stuck it in her purse.

"I do! That's why I volunteered today. My friend was supposed to come, but she had a family emergency, so I told her I'd come in her place." Mya shuffled some papers around on the table. "But I love it. I'm almost a completely different person since I got here. You get so much freedom in college, but the people here really know how to support you."

"See, that's what I'm looking for," Nia said. "A lot of these other schools are just way too big. I don't want to be in a class with 500 other people."

"My biggest class has about 50 people," Mya said. "But that's pretty rare. So I feel you on not wanting to be invisible."

"Plus, I'm not so sure I want to go that far away," Nia admitted. "I think I'd miss my little brother. And my mom and dad too, of course."

Mya nodded. "You sound like me! That's why I went to Spelman. Only about half an hour away from my family. I'm a daddy's girl."

"Me too!"

"Okay, are we twins or something? We related? I mean, we definitely look like it," Mya joked. She gestured to Nia's phone. "I'm going to give you my number. You have any questions about Spelman? You can text me. I hope I'll see you on campus next year."

"You might," Nia replied. She handed Mya her phone and watched as she typed her number in.

"I'm going to walk around for a bit but I'll definitely text you. It was so good to talk to you today."

"Same here. And I mean it. If you have any questions, I can be like your big sister guide."

Nia smiled. "I appreciate that. I'll see you later?"

"See ya," Mya said, turning to talk to another young girl who had walked up to the table.

Nia looked around the busy gym and gathered all the materials in her arms. *I think I'm done*, she said to herself. *Time to go home.*

As she turned to find the exit, she ran into her friend April heading right toward her. "Hey girl!" She leaned in and gave her a hug. "You about to leave?"

Nia gestured to the folders and brochures in her hands. "Yup. I think I hit all the tables I wanted to hit. You?"

"I just gotta drop this raffle ticket off and then I'm leaving. Can I get a ride with you? My dad dropped me off."

"Yeah, no problem."

"Okay, great – I'll be right back." Before Nia could even make it out of the gym, April had caught up with her.

"That lady from Spelman was really nice," she said, brushing her hair out of her face. "She had me seriously thinking about going there."

"You mean Mya?" Nia asked. *Now where is the car*? She was always forgetting where she parked.

"You know her name? Dang," April said, laughing. "I thought I was doing good by remembering what school she was representing."

Nia laughed. "I just introduced myself and she told me her name. She actually went to Mays too."

"That's what's up," April said, sliding into the passenger seat. "I thought she looked familiar."

"Yeah, she's Caleb's older sister."

"Caleb with the dimples? Caleb with the 4.0 GPA and the muscles to match?" April rolled down her window to let some of the cooler September air in. "Can we go back and tell Mya to hook us up?"

"I'm sure Mya don't want to be hooking thirsty girls up with her brother."

"I'm not thirsty; I'm ready," April said, laughing again.

Nia pulled out of the parking lot and shook her head. "Ready for what?"

"Girl, never mind," April replied, "I know Caleb doesn't go for my type."

"And what's your type?"

"You know – goofy, silly, crazy," April said. "He likes those 'pretty girls' who spend all weekend in Sephora."

"What's wrong with being one of those girls?"

"Nothing's wrong with it," April shrugged "It's just not me."

They drove in silence for a few minutes.

As high school wore on, Nia found herself spending more time with Patrice and less time with April.

It wasn't intentional; April was a three-sport athlete—she was in track, basketball and volleyball and hardly had time to hang out anymore. When she did have free time, she usually spent it with her teammates. Nia was busy too as president of student council. Their schedules just never seemed to match up, so when they had time alone, it could be kind of awkward.

April broke the silence first. "Are you going to apply to Spelman?"

"Not yet. I could be planning on it though. Are you?"

She nodded. "Of course. My mom would be pissed if I didn't. You know practically every woman in my family graduated from Spelman—my grandmother, my mom, all my aunts. They roll *deep*."

"But do *you* want to go there?"

"I guess so," she said, picking at invisible lint on her leggings. "I'm applying to Howard too."

"You want to go to D.C.?"

"I kind of want to get out of Atlanta," April admitted. "Been here all my life. I'd love to go someplace new, where I don't know anybody or anything."

"That's so scary to me!" Nia said. "You're not scared about being alone in a new city?"

"Nope," April said. "Don't you want to go see someplace new?"

"Nah, I'm good," Nia said. "That's too much change all at once. If I'm going to college and living on my own, I gotta at least know the city."

April shook her head. "I'm tired of the same ol' streets, the same people, the same Peachtree everything. I don't wanna hear about any more peaches!"

The two of them laughed.

"Patrice is thinking about going to Howard too," Nia said. "Y'all are both trying to leave me!"

"That would be dope if we both ended up there," April said. She took a long pause and then added, "I feel like Patrice has been avoiding me lately, though."

"Why do you say that?"

"Come on, girl. I hardly ever see you two anymore."

"You never see us? How about we never see you, Miss-I-play-all-the-sports-all-the-time."

April chuckled. "I can't help it if I want to use these long legs for something other than strutting down the hall at school. I'm trying to get that scholarship money."

"I feel you. I'm stressing about that right now."

"About how much it costs?"

"Yeah," Nia admitted. "I don't know if I'm going to be getting as many scholarships as my parents were hoping for. And then I keep hearing about how everybody's graduating college with all these loans. It's scary."

"But we'll make it through. Everybody does. We just gotta do the best we can."

"You're right," she said as she pulled onto April's street. "It'll all work out."

"Of course it will."

They both got out of the car and Nia gave April a strong hug goodbye. "We gotta hang out together more. I miss you, girl."

April squeezed her back. "I miss you too! It hasn't been the same without you in my classes, walking home together like we used to back in seventh grade. Remember that?"

"I do!" They laughed for a few more minutes and Nia remembered how much fun she used to have hanging out with Patrice and April and made a promise to herself that they would have to get together to hang out before they were spread all over the country at college.

"You want to come in?" April asked, gesturing to the house.

"Nah, I've got to get home." Nia jiggled her keys and put her hand on the driver's door. "I'm supposed to take my brother to baseball practice."

"He's playing baseball again this year, huh?"

"Yeah, he really likes it." Nia considered keeping the conversation going for a few more minutes but decided against it. "Well, I'll see you later. Text me, girl. I miss you."

April just smiled and turned to go into the house.

After Nia had taken PJ to baseball practice, she was beat. She slipped off her shoes and socks and stretched out on the couch. Her mom was working late again (she had been putting in overtime ever since Nia's senior year started) and wasn't going to be home until well past PJ's bedtime. Luckily, PJ was old enough that the evening routine wasn't that tough for her.

"Did you take your shower?" Nia asked, after PJ popped downstairs only 10 minutes after she had told him to go wash up.

"Yeah," PJ said, flopping on the couch next to her. His skin looked a little damp, but Nia knew better than to take his word for it.

She leaned in and sniffed his armpits. "Ew, boy, did you get under your arms?"

"I did!" he said, pulling his arms tight against his sides.

"Did you use soap?"

"Yes! Dang, Nia."

"It doesn't smell like it. Go try that again." She waved him up the stairs and she heard him mumble under his breath as he headed to the bathroom again.

Nia closed her eyes again and put her head on one of the decorative pillows on the couch. It was only 9 p.m. and she felt like it might as well be midnight. Senior year was killing her, with deadlines for this and that every other day. School was much harder, precisely because she had less time to devote to it. She had just been hired as an after school tutor at her old middle school of all places.

She was glad to be able to earn some money to hopefully save for college, but worried that adding one more thing to her busy schedule would make it hard to keep her grades up.

Even with all of her activities, she managed to get mostly A's and B's, and she really wanted to keep it that way.

Her phone buzzed and took her out of her thoughts. The text was from her mom: *On my way. Be there in 10 minutes. Can you heat up some dinner for me?*

Nia heaved herself off the couch and went to the kitchen. Humming softly to herself, she grabbed a plate from the cabinet, then took the leftovers out of the refrigerator.

She scooped out some macaroni and cheese, baked chicken and sweet potatoes, and popped them into the microwave, drumming her fingers on the counter as she watched the numbers tick down.

When her mom got home, Nia heard her drop her purse onto the table by the entryway and head straight for the kitchen. Her mother went to the microwave, nodded her thanks to Nia, then sat down and started eating without even taking off her jacket. She closed her eyes and let out a low moan of enjoyment. "This is so good," she said. "I haven't eaten all day. I'm starving."

Nia sat down across from her mom, looking worried. "Mom, are you working all this overtime...for me? Because I'll be leaving next year?"

Her mother took another bite of the macaroni and cheese and swallowed before answering. "What? Why are you asking me that?"

"Because I feel bad that you're working so much," Nia said, looking down at her hands.

"Ah, so that's what this is about." Her mom wiped her mouth and grabbed Nia's hands. "Baby, my job is to take care of you. And that's what I'm trying to do. Your dad and I have been talking and we know that we can't afford to pay for all of your tuition. But that doesn't mean that I won't do my best to make sure you have what you need for school. No need to worry. I'm the adult. I know how much I can handle."

Nia nodded. "Okay. I just felt bad because I know you have PJ and all his baseball stuff and there's a lot going on right now."

"Yeah, but it's nothing we can't handle." Her mom picked up her fork again and continued eating. "You are going to do great things. You think about *that*. Let me worry about the rest of it."

***

The next day, Nia thought about cancelling her date with Brandon. She still liked him, but she felt like she needed a break. Ever since they had officially gotten back together at the beginning of senior year, he was no longer shy about telling her he was ready to have sex.

Watching Patrice's drama with Marcus unfold—Marcus eventually came clean that he wasn't a virgin and had had sex with other girls before Patrice —left Nia afraid to trust Brandon, even though she had known him since middle school.

Patrice shook her head when Nia told her that Brandon wanted to have sex. "Girl, don't believe these boys. They will say anything."

Nia thought Brandon was different, but she had to admit that she didn't like the back and forth they had at the end of every date.

She was running out of ways to tell him that she wanted to wait and felt like he was growing more and more impatient.

She decided to get dressed and meet him at the game anyway. It was a big rival's game; Nia was rooting for her school to beat Brandon's school. No matter what the outcome was, they were going for burgers afterward. Nia insisted on driving herself because, as her mom taught her, she didn't want to be dependent on someone else for a ride. Having her own car meant she could always determine when she would leave.

When she got there, Brandon had a pocket full of her favorite candy, Now & Laters, which she happily accepted. He could drive her crazy, but he had a habit of doing small things that made her happy to have a boyfriend who was thoughtful.

He draped his arm around her shoulders. "You cold?" he asked.

"A little, but I'll be okay," she said, sorting through the candy to eat her favorite flavors first.

He rubbed her shoulders and turned his attention to the game. Mays led 21-14 at the half, and Nia was getting hungry. The candy, while delicious, was not filling. She knew Brandon had been waiting for this game all week, so she went and grabbed some snacks to get her through the second half.

"Hey, Nia!" Patrice said, finding her in line at concessions. "I thought you'd be here."

"Yeah, everybody's here," Nia said, looking at the packed stands.

"*Everybody*," Patrice said, rolling her eyes. "Including Marcus."

"Where?" Nia turned to look around and Patrice grabbed her arm, silently willing her to be still.

"He's here and he's with some girl," Patrice said, getting visibly angry. "Hope she's got good insurance. She's gonna need it, messing with him."

"Oh come on," Nia said, chomping on some nachos to soothe her hungry stomach. "You said the doctor told you most guys don't even have any symptoms, so he probably didn't even know he had it, Patrice."

Patrice held up a hand to stop her friend from talking. "What?"

"I mean, maybe he didn't lie to you. Maybe he really didn't know he had it."

"So that makes giving me a disease okay?" she whispered through clenched teeth. She looked around to make sure no one was paying attention to their conversation.

"No, it doesn't," Nia said. "I'm just saying…."

Patrice closed her eyes tight. "Girl, whose side are you on?"

"I'm on your side, always."

"Then act like it," Patrice snapped. "I don't want to talk about this now. I'll see you later." She huffed and turned away, heading to the opposite side of the stadium.

Nia stood there dumbfounded, aware that this was the first time she'd had a fight with Patrice. She headed back to the stands where Brandon was sitting.

"Everything good?" he asked, when he saw her face. The expression on her face must have given away how she felt.

"Yeah, just ran into Patrice and had an argument." She shook her head. "I'll text her later."

Brandon nodded and swiped some nachos from Nia, then went back to watching the game. An hour later, Mays had won, 35-24, and Brandon was in a good mood even though his school lost. "You want to go to Grindhouse?" he asked, as he held her hand and walked her to her car. "I'll meet you there."

"Alright, I'll see you there in a few minutes."

They kissed goodbye and somehow, Brandon made it to the restaurant before Nia. "I already ordered your favorite," he said, smiling wide.

"Turkey burger with cheddar and grilled onions? Yup. Your man pays attention."

"Thank you. This means you paid too, right?" Nia joked.

"I ain't say all that," Brandon said, laughing at her.

Soon their order arrived and they ate in silence for a few minutes. "This is so good," Nia said. She pulled some of the grilled onions off her burger and ate them separately. "Thanks for meeting me here."

"Well, you know, I try to keep you happy," he said, his brown eyes twinkling.

"That you do." She leaned over at the table and kissed him on the cheek.

"So where do you want to go after this?" He dipped his fries in the big pool of ketchup. "We could go back to my house. I got that new Kevin Hart movie."

"It's out already?"

He nodded.

"Okay, that'll be fun."

They finished eating and Nia smiled the whole way over to Brandon's house. *This is probably one of our best dates,* she realized. *And to think I almost wasn't going to come.*

After Nia said hi to his mom, who quietly went upstairs after greeting her, the two of them got comfortable in the basement, where the big TV was. They cuddled together on the couch and watched a comedy special. They both laughed at all the same parts, almost wheezing by the time the credits rolled.

"He is so crazy," Nia said, wiping the tears from her eyes. "Ugh, that was too funny."

"Right?" Brandon leaned back on the couch and brought his hands to his sides.

"What do you want to do? You want to watch another movie?"

Nia checked her phone for the time. It was after 11, and her midnight curfew was going to be here before she knew it. "Nah, I've got to leave soon."

"Well in that case...." Brandon gently lifted Nia's head to his and kissed her on the lips. Nia melted, as she always did, and kissed him back harder.

His eyes roamed all over her body and she felt herself getting warm to the touch. He kissed her while caressing her back and her thighs. He lifted her shirt up and, sensing no resistance, pulled it up over her head. This was as far as they had ever gotten before and she could tell by how he was breathing that Brandon was excited.

They continued kissing on the couch, Brandon easing Nia back until he was hovering over her. He fiddled in his pocket for something and a few seconds later pulled out a blue condom wrapper. Nia heard the foil crinkle and opened her eyes.

"What is that for?" she asked, her face turning sour.

"For protection," he said, not picking up on her disapproval. He went in to kiss her again but this time Nia turned her head.

"I told you, I'm not ready yet," she said. She pushed him backward a bit and sat up. She found her shirt on the floor and gathered it in her lap.

He sighed heavily and put his head in his hands. "And when do you think you'll *be* ready?"

"I don't know!" she said, frustrated. "I just don't understand why we can't just..."

"Just what?"

"Kiss and stuff," she finished. "Why do you always have to go straight to sex?"

"Because I want to have sex," he said plainly. "And I want to have sex with *you.*"

Now it was Nia's turn to sigh. "I'm just not ready. I mean, you see what Patrice and Marcus just went through. Aren't you scared?"

"We're not Patrice and Marcus," he reminded her. "I haven't been with anybody else. And neither have you."

"That's just what Marcus said too," Nia said under her breath but loud enough for Brandon to hear her clearly.

"So now you don't believe me?" Brandon said, looking hurt.

"I'm just saying...boys say whatever to get what they want."

"I'm not lying to you," Brandon insisted. "I love you."

"And I love you too."

"So..." he held up the condom wrapper. "We have a condom. We've never been with anybody else. The worst that could happen is the condom could break."

"That's a big worst-that-could-happen."

"But it won't happen." He looked at the condom. "It's brand-new. I got it from my brother's stash."

"Stop trying to talk me into this. I said I wasn't ready."

"You scared it will hurt?"

She put her head in her hands. "You're not listening to me."

"I *am* listening. You said you're scared. I'm trying to tell you there's nothing to be afraid of."

Nia grabbed her shirt and slipped it back on over her head, effectively shutting down whatever hope Brandon had for losing his virginity that night.

He sighed. "So when do you think you'll be ready? 'Cause I can't keep doing this whole kiss-then-you-get-uncomfortable thing."

"What are you saying?"

"I'm saying you need to make up your mind," Brandon said, throwing up his hands. "Either you want to have sex or you don't."

"I just told you I don't."

"Well, that's it then." He picked up the remote and turned off the TV.

They sat there for a few minutes without saying anything. After a while, they heard the footsteps of his mother in the room above them as she came back downstairs to the kitchen.

"I think I'm going to leave," Nia said, grabbing her purse off the side table.

"Okay," he said simply. He didn't get up to walk her out but instead kept fiddling with the remote.

"Well, I'll see you later then," she said as she reached the bottom of the steps. "Are you going to walk me out?"

He sighed and got up, brushing past her to lead the way upstairs.

Brandon's mom was in the kitchen as they got to the first floor. "You're leaving?" she said, squeezing Nia. "I hope you'll come back soon, okay?"

Nia squeezed her back, looking over her shoulder at Brandon, who was fiddling with his hoodie's drawstring and trying not to make eye contact with Nia. "Yeah, I will," she lied. She knew that this was probably the last time she'd be over there.

She got to her car and Brandon stood on the porch, ready for her to pull off. "I'll see you later?"

He nodded, but didn't speak. She shook her head, waved goodbye dismissively and got in the car.

Patrice's words echoed in her ear: *These boys will say anything.*

Was it true? Was Brandon done with her just because she didn't want to have sex?

Nia decided to make her own choice. She was done with *him.* She had a lot to think about—college, the rest of senior year, her new job—and worrying about whether a boy liked her had never been her style. He was a nice guy, but there had to be plenty more nice guys in her future, especially at college. *Let me just focus on getting there,* she thought to herself.

***

Oh, please don't let me be late my first day of work, Nia pleaded quietly as she thumped the steering wheel. A stalled car in the left lane had traffic backed up, and Nia was dreading the feeling of sheepishly walking in fifteen minutes late when she hadn't even officially started.

Her new job as an after school counselor at her old middle school had been set up by Ms. Jimenez, her old art teacher.

When the district got an unexpected contribution from an anonymous donor, Ms. Jimenez was quick to suggest they use it to develop an art program for the students who needed a safe space to be after school versus heading home where there was no adult supervision. Ms. Jimenez tapped Nia and some other former students to come in and act as counselors in the program. They were each assigned four children to help with homework, do projects, and teach them about life as high school students. It paid just enough for Nia to feel like she could save a little for college and still have a little fun with the rest.

Nia pulled into the school parking lot and glanced at her phone. 3:27 on the dot. She needed to be there at 3:30, and she would have to sprint to make it inside on time. *Good thing I wore my Nikes*, she thought as she parked and took off for the back entrance.

She was out of breath by the time she reached the gym, where the program was going to be held. Ms. Jimenez saw Nia run in and came over to give her a hug.

"I'm so happy you're here," she said, smiling widely.

"I would have been here earlier but I ran into traffic," Nia replied, trying to catch her breath and look a bit more professional. "Thank you for allowing me to be a part of this program."

"Of course. We're just about to get started." Ms. Jimenez draped an arm over Nia's shoulders and walked her over to the group, which was getting set up at a few tables in the center of the room. "Everyone, this is Nia." She gestured to the other counselors. "Nia, this is Danielle, Sharice, Damita, and Jason." They all gave a wave and went back to the task at hand, fixing the snacks for the students.

"What should I do?" Nia asked, taking off her backpack and setting it down along the wall.

Ms. Jimenez checked her watch. "The students will be down in about ten minutes, so jump in here and help get the snack table together. Damita can tell you what we'll be doing next. I have to run to the office and make sure they dismiss the students to the gym and not to the cafeteria, which is where we were supposed to be originally."

Damita popped her head up at the mention of her name and waved Nia over. "Hey girl," she said, giving her a quick hug.

Nia remembered her from a few classes back in middle school but they didn't talk much then. "So basically, we're just getting everything open and making sure everybody has a snack bag. Ms. Jimenez didn't want them to start hungry so we're going to feed them first. Then we're going to make little art collages so we can get to know the kids. Some of them are really struggling so we have to figure out how we can help them."

Nia nodded. "Okay, I can help with that."

For the next three hours, Nia bonded with each of her four students. She was in awe of how young they seemed, their cheeks still round with baby fat. She was happy to be spending her afternoons doing something that seemed to be helping people. She wished something like this had existed when she was in middle school.

Before she realized it, the last of the students had been picked up and it was time to break down the tables and clean up.

"So how do you think the first day went?" Ms. Jimenez asked them, picking up scrap pieces of construction paper and putting them in her paper bin to reuse at the next session.

"I really liked my group," Nia said. "They are a great bunch of kids."

Danielle nodded. "Yeah, mine were a little quiet at first but I think this is a great idea. I'm glad so many signed up!" Sharice agreed. "One of my kids, Demetrius, had me cracking up all afternoon."

Jason grabbed a stack of used paper plates off the table and tossed them in the trash. "Oh, Meech? He lives on my street —it's good he's here."

Ms. Jimenez smiled in response. "Good. I'm glad you all get what we're doing here. I think you all are the perfect group for these kids. It's good for them to see you – young students that used to go to this same school, now heading off to college. You'll be good role models for them."

They shuffled around making sure the gym was spotless before they closed up. One by one they left, until it was just Nia and Ms. Jimenez.

"So how is school going?" Ms. Jimenez asked, pulling her keys out of her purse. Somehow, they had ended up parking close to each other so they headed to their cars together.

"Busy," Nia said, stretching her arms toward the sky. She had been bent over working on an art projects with her kids and needed to get the stiffness out of her back. "Very busy; senior year is no joke."

Ms. Jimenez chuckled. "I bet. But you've always been one of those students who thrive under pressure. So I don't doubt that you'll do great this year and in college.

"Have you thought about which schools you're applying to?"

"So far, I've got Spelman, Emory, and University of Georgia."

"Those are all great schools! Man, time really flies. I remember having you in art class and you were so young, so studious. And now you're about to head to college. You kids make me feel old."

Nia looked at Ms. Jimenez in her sky-high purple heels and cute black pencil skirt. "At least you don't look old," Nia joked.

"Well, bless your heart for that," Ms. Jimenez said, laughing. "Good thing black don't crack, right?"

She gave Nia a hug and hit the key fob to unlock her car door. "I'll see you tomorrow, same time. Get some sleep! It's going to be a busy afternoon."

Let's Talk – College Readiness

For as long as I could remember, the expectation was that I was going to go to college.

My parents were big advocates of education, and they wanted me to have all the opportunities that lay ahead of me. I understand that for a lot of young people, college isn't necessarily a given, especially if you would be the first in your family to attend. It can seem so unrealistic for you, as college tuition is so incredibly expensive and if your family doesn't have a lot of money, how will you pay for it?

However, the costs of not going to college are high as well. Research shows that people with a college degree will make, on average, far more than those who only have a high school diploma. Having a college degree will also help you get (and keep!) a job in a bad economy more easily than a high school graduate. Most jobs, particularly those in the decades to come, will require some form of higher education before you can even get in the door, so making the decision to go to college will only benefit you down the line.

But let's not kid ourselves — college comes with a steep price tag. Nia felt her parents worry about how much college would cost, and you see all of them working overtime trying to make it happen. The good news is that there are several ways to pay for college, allowing you to focus on your coursework.

Contrary to what you might believe, paying for college begins in high school. If you want the best shot at lowering your costs for college, it's up to you to start thinking about that now, before you even apply to the schools of your choice. Share this chapter with your parents so you can all get on the same page about your future. Here's a rundown of prepping for college, no matter where you are in the process:

Junior year

Your freshman and sophomore years of high school are important, but college prep gets real during junior year. This is when you start looking at everything you've done so far in high school and you kick it up a notch.

This is the last full year that college admissions officers have for evaluating how well you might fit in at their school, so make it count.

Don't go it alone

Talk with your school's guidance counselor about your classes so you can make sure your transcript will look desirable.

Some schools won't admit you without a certain number of courses in math, science and foreign language, so be sure you're checking in to make sure you hit all the requirements. Your guidance counselor should also have information for you about schools you're interested in, so you can plan college visits or see if they will be attending a college fair near you (more on those later!).

Take the Test

You may not be a fan of standardized tests, but in order to get into college, you have to take either the ACT or SAT. It may not be fair (you could be one of those students who does better in coursework than on tests), but that's how colleges evaluate students across the board. Get the dates for the tests early in the year, as you'll need to register several weeks in advance. You can also take these tests your senior year, but it's good to get a sense of where you score as a junior and then be able to take the test again as a senior if you want to try to increase your score. Look around your community for free or low-cost test preparation programs that you can attend in person or look for some resources online. Khan Academy offers free practice tests at www.khanacademy.org/sat.

Get Involved

Colleges look for well-rounded students —those who do well in their classes but also have experience in school clubs, sports, or community groups. Take a minute to write down all the activities you could include on your college application. If the list feels a little short, consider joining some activities at school or taking on some volunteer opportunities. VolunteerMatch.org is a good place to start.

Do Your Research

Where do you want to go to college? Are you more like Nia, who wants to stay closer to home, where things are familiar? Or are you more like April, ready to start your adult life in a new space? Whichever way you're leaning, start compiling a list of colleges you're interested in. Consider more than just the financial cost. While some schools have outrageous tuition (I mean more than $50,000 each year!), some of these same schools have great financial aid offers for students who don't have wealthy parents, so don't count them out yet. Find out which school might be the best fit and then think about how you could pay for it. Spend some time on the school website and its social media pages to see what student life is like, and if you can picture yourself being a student there.

Take Advantage of College Fairs

College fairs are the perfect opportunity to get out and talk to people from a variety of schools all in one day. Colleges will often have current students or alumni at the tables, so you can ask them questions that you might not ask an admissions counselor or staff member.

Get a Real Look at the Schools

Junior year is a great time to begin planning college visits. There's something about being on the campus that can let you know whether the school would be a good fit for you. Where are the students hanging out? Is the library busy? Is it a crowded campus or are the buildings spread out with lots of green space? You can arrange to have an official tour guide through the admissions office or you can visit and walk through the campus on your own.

For the official college tours, they usually have a current student leading a group through campus, hitting all the major spots (a residence hall, the library, student center, classroom buildings, etc.). They are paid to get you interested in the school, but ask questions if they didn't address something you're curious about or if something they've mentioned doesn't sound right to you.

Spend Your Summer Wisely

Having a job will not only put money in your pocket, but it will also help college admissions staff see that you are a student who will be able to excel at doing two things at once. If you've spent some time thinking about what you might want to do for a career (see the *What You Should Know* section at the end of this chapter for a career-planning writing exercise), see if there is any available opportunity for you to do an internship at a company in a related field. For example, if you want to be a veterinarian, look up a local clinic and see if they have volunteer opportunities.

Senior year

Senior year is when decisions have to be made – both by you and the colleges and universities you're interested in. Because this year has a lot more on your to-do list, we're going to break this down month by month so you can see at a glance how you conquer these tasks.

September – Get Ready

First things first—double-check that you are on track to graduate! I can't tell you how crushing it is to think you can walk with your class only to find out that you are missing credits or don't have the right credits to graduate. Don't let that happen to you; find out early where you stand so you have time to make it right if need be.

Take the SAT and/or ACT if you didn't take it as a junior, or if you want to improve your score. By now you should have an idea of the score you're aiming for, which depends on the schools you're applying to. Regardless, with both the SAT and ACT, the higher you can score, the better.

The next thing to do is get yourself organized. The last thing you want to do is miss out on the chance of going to the college of your dreams because you were unorganized and missed a deadline. Once you have a list of the schools you'd like to apply to, consider all of the different pieces of information you will need to have on hand—transcripts, test scores, applications, letters of recommendation, etc. There are programs you can use to keep all of this straight in your calendar. One tool, called BOLD Guidance, allows you to select the schools you're interested in and breaks down the application process into small, easy steps.

It even sends you reminders when items are due so you won't overlook them!

This is also a good time to request recommendation letters from teachers, school counselors, or employers. To make it easy for them, it is best to give them a stamped, addressed envelope (ready to be sent to the college of your choice), along with your transcripts and any information about your extracurricular activities. If you have to send in more than one recommendation letter, try to get people who have seen you in different environments — your English teacher and your basketball coach, for example.

October

It is time to fill out the FAFSA (Free Application for Federal Student Aid).

You want to be sure you file the form as soon after October 1st as possible. This will help you see what your family will be expected to contribute and will guide your decisions moving forward. If your parents make under a certain of amount of annual income, colleges and universities take that into consideration, allowing for a larger financial aid package. You will need to complete the FAFSA to be eligible for federal loans, grants or scholarships, so don't delay!

In the past, most students didn't apply to college until their spring semester, but now, some colleges offer early admission in the fall semester. Gather all your materials so you won't have to scramble and again, be aware of deadlines and any fees you may have to pay.

Most schools will ask that you submit an essay with your application, and when I speak to young women, this is the item that freaks them out the most. I try to remind them (and now I'm reminding *you*) that this essay does not need to be perfect. It needs to follow any instructions given, and it needs to read well, but there is no perfect answer. Take a deep breath, and do your best!

If you're applying to multiple schools and the application fees begin to add up, you can talk to your guidance counselor to request a fee waiver.

October is also a fantastic month to research scholarships. At this point, this should be one of your main priorities. A lot of students rely on student loans to help pay for school and don't spend enough time searching for scholarships they may be eligible for.

The beauty of scholarships and grants is that they don't have to be paid back! That's 100% free and clear money that you can use for school costs. You don't have to necessarily be at the top of your class to win scholarships. So many students mistakenly think that because they're not a top athlete or don't have a 4.0 GPA that they can't get scholarships. That's false! There are scholarships for everything under the sun. Did you know there is a scholarship that grants you free housing if you have a twin who also attends the school? You just never know until you research, so get started!

Let everyone know you are looking for scholarships and ask them to do some of the legwork for you. Look at scholarship opportunities at the colleges you're applying to, but also ask your guidance counselor and your local church.

Also remember that all scholarship information is available for free online, so if you find a website that asks you to pay, it's a scam and beware!

November

If you're planning to apply for early decision, finalize your applications and get them ready to be sent. It never hurts to have a parent or counselor review them to make sure there's nothing missing.

December

If you're not applying for early decision, this is the time to organize regular decision applications and financial aid forms, because they will be due in January and/or February. Items you may need:

- Application forms
- Registration fees
- Letters of recommendation
- Transcripts
- Test scores
- Essay

January

Ask your guidance office in January to send first semester transcripts to schools where you applied. At the end of the school year, they will need to send final transcripts to the college you will attend.

February/March/April

Most of your senior year has been consumed with applications, scholarships and deadlines, but it's also important to remember that you still need to excel in your classes! Don't slack off and think you can coast your final year. Your grades still matter, and colleges will see your final transcripts with your grades from your senior year.

It is this time of year that you will receive your acceptance letters and financial aid offers. Take a minute to congratulate yourself on making it this far in the process! Review your financial aid packages, and work with your parents to select the right fit for you.

May

Once you have received offer letters, May 1 is typically the deadline for letting colleges know you plan to attend. This is when you also need to make a deposit, so be aware of that. You will also need to accept any financial aid offers (please don't slack on this step!). Also, you can notify the other schools you were accepted to, that you will not be attending.

What You Should Know – Planning for College and Beyond

Go to my website ***www.drkelahenry.com/resources*** for a list of everything from scholarship help to non-profits that assist students with making the transition to college.

5 Possible Colleges/Universities That I'm Interested In

1.

2.

3.

4.

5.

5 Possible Majors That I'm Interested In

1.

2.

3.

4.

5.

5 Possible Careers That I'm Interested In

1.

2.

3.

4.

5.

5 Must-Haves For A College/University I Attend

1.

2.

3.

4.

5.

Chapter Seven: 1881 Spelman College

"I'm so glad you're here!" Mya said, rushing up to Nia and giving her a big hug. "Does it seem like a year ago that we met?"

Nia relaxed a bit into Mya's embrace and smiled. "Not at all."

The hustle and bustle of Spelman's move-in day made Nia incredibly nervous, but having Mya take time out to meet her and help her get settled meant a lot to her. Since they'd met at the college fair the previous year, Mya had been like a big sister of sorts. She'd sat down with Nia and helped with her college essays and brought her to campus so she could get a *real* look at the school, beyond what the campus tour guides would mention.

When Nia had gotten her acceptance letter, the second person she'd called (after her dad, of course) was Mya.

"I'm so proud of you!" Mya had squealed into the phone. "I knew you'd get in but now it's official! Congratulations, lil' sis." That night, Mya had driven from campus to take Nia to Paschal's in celebration.

Nia discovered shortly after her acceptance that April had gotten into Spelman as well. With a legacy as deep and wide as April's, there was little doubt, but knowing that officially she would have two friends on campus helped Nia feel more relaxed about the transition to college. Patrice, who had been accepted at all fifteen colleges she applied to, chose to go to Howard, which stung a bit for April, who had wanted to leave Atlanta but couldn't go against three generations of Spelman family members.

Once acceptance letters were out, the remainder of senior year had been a blur. The time between getting in and moving in seemed like an eternity, with Nia obsessively checking lists of what freshmen were allowed to bring. She'd had a ball with her mom in Target, tossing new sheets, shower caddies, toiletries, and of course, hair products in the cart—she had to make sure her twist-outs could flourish on campus. She made an agreement with her mom that she would pay half, but once they got to the cash register, her eyes had opened wide at the total.

Her mom had laughed at her daughter's expression. "Welcome to adulthood."

Now they had packed up both her mother's van and her dad's car and headed to campus to get Nia moved in two days before classes started.

"Well, let's get you moved in," Mya said, turning around to head toward where Nia's parents were waiting. "You'll love it here at Manley."

They walked to the van where Nia's mom was sweating and wiping her brow. "I don't know how we got all this stuff jammed in here," she said. "You probably won't even need all of this!"

"Probably won't," Mya agreed, eyeing the mountain of plastic bins piled high in the backseat. "But every freshman packs too much. That is normal."

"Had so much stuff we had to leave my little brother at home," Nia joked.

Nia's mom gave Mya a hug. "Thank you for helping my Nia. I feel much better about having her leave me knowing that you're here to watch out for her."

Mya slung an arm around Nia's shoulders. "Of course! I've always got to look out for my lil' sis!"

Nia's dad came up the walkway, sweat beading across his forehead. "It *would* be 88 degrees today, wouldn't it?" He nodded hello to Mya. "I'm parked down a bit further. That's as close as I could get. It's a madhouse today."

"That's okay," Mya said. "I can get you a couple carts to help you load up all the stuff. I'll be right back."

Five minutes later, Mya returned with two tan carts and the four of them unloaded the two vehicles and took all of Nia's new belongings up to her second floor room in Manley Hall.

"You got a room by yourself?" Mya asked, looking around at the empty bed on the other side of the room.

"No, my roommate's just not here yet," Nia said, pulling her phone out of her pocket to double-check her roommate assignment. "Her name is Tamara, I think."

"Cool. Well, you gotta make sure you keep your stuff to one side of the room so you don't start off on the wrong foot," Mya advised. "She comes in and sees your stuff all over the place and you're gonna have a problem."

"Makes sense," Nia said. She turned to her parents, who were red in the face and exhausted. "Thanks for helping me move in."

"You sound like you're trying to get rid of us," her dad teased. He turned to his ex-wife. "Doesn't it sound like it, Sabrina?"

"Sure does," her mom said. She squeezed Nia tight for a full 30 seconds. "I can't believe my baby is all grown up."

"It's okay, mom," Nia said, patting her mom on the arm as a signal that she could let go.

Mya clasped her hands and brought them up to meet her chin. "Aww, this is so cute. You want me to take a picture of you three?"

Nia's dad patted his pockets. "I can't believe we almost forgot to get a picture!"

He handed the phone to Mya and stood next to his daughter, her mom on the other side.

"That's a perfect picture," Mya said, handing the phone back.

"Yeah it is," Nia's dad agreed. He gestured toward Sabrina. "Okay, well, we will get out of your hair, then." He kissed Nia on the forehead and gave her a strong hug. "Make good decisions, okay? I'm proud of you."

"Thanks, dad." Nia took a deep breath and walked them out. When she got back to the room, Mya was sitting on the desk, swinging her legs.

"I'm gonna head out too," Mya said. "Just wanted to make sure you got settled in okay. I've got a few other errands to run before school starts and I bet the stores are full of freshman like you who had to make a last-minute dash to buy stuff."

"Where are you staying this year?" Nia asked, moving a box off her bed and looking around for the box that contained the sheets and pillows.

"This is actually my first year living off campus," Mya said. "I found this dope apartment on Piedmont and went in on it with two friends. So that'll be…interesting."

"You're gonna leave me here to unpack all this by myself?" Nia whined, only half joking.

"Yes, lil' sis, you're on your own." Mya gave her a salute and headed for the door. "You got this. I believe in you."

Nia was about halfway done unpacking when she heard the door to her dorm room. In walked a girl she assumed was Tamara, struggling under the weight of a heavy box.

She put the box down with a loud thump on the empty desk across the room. Nia let her catch her breath for a moment and then got up to introduce herself.

"I'm Nia," she said, extending her hand for a handshake.

"I'm Tamara, but you can call me Tami," her roommate replied, skipping the handshake and going in for a hug. "Sorry, I'm a hugger. Hope you don't mind."

"Oh," Nia said, caught off guard. "Not at all."

"Okay, I have two more boxes in the car and then I'll be all done," she said.

She shifted her cross body bag and patted her hair. "This weave is gonna slide right out if I keep sweating this much."

Nia laughed. "Are your parents bringing them up?"

"No, no parents," Tami said. She paused and said softly, "Just me today. My parents, they died when I was younger."

Nia felt her face get hot with embarrassment. *I can't believe I just said that*, she thought as she stumbled to find the right words.

"Oh, I'm sorry for assuming," she finally said.

Tami waved her hand. "That's okay. I'm fine now. I've been in foster care since I was eleven. Bounced around from home to home after that. I've learned to pack light."

Nia suddenly felt embarrassed to have brought so much stuff to campus and awkwardly gestured to all her belongings. "I should have learned that lesson."

"I see," Tami said, laughing. "Be glad you didn't have to learn that lesson."

"You need help with the last two boxes?"

"I'd love that. Then I won't have to make two trips!"

Together they headed down the crowded hallway, different sounds and scents filling the air. Through the propped-open doors, Nia could see a collection of women getting settled in the dorms—from the natural-haired like herself, rocking gorgeous locs, afros and long, chunky braids, to the weaved up and relaxed women, wearing long, silky hair. It made Nia feel like she could fit in around here. Every type of African American woman was represented on campus. Nia wasn't sure what to expect in college, but so far, so good.

When Mya said the college was like one big sisterhood, she wasn't lying. After being on campus only a few days, Nia had already made friends who felt like family. First there was Tami, who had become one of Nia's closest friends. Even though Nia had grown up partially in a single parent household, she was still privileged in many ways. She had no clue about some of the harsh realities of the real world. Tami had seen it all and had experienced the worst, but still managed to have so much optimism for the future. She was teaching Nia how to stand up for herself and own her womanhood.

Then there was Felicia, who roomed with April down in Abby Hall. She was always cracking jokes and laughing, which is why she got along with April so well. She was the eldest of nine kids, so sharing a bathroom with dozens of women on the floor was no big deal to Felicia. "It's cleaner than my bathroom at home," she joked.

Nia had settled on biology as a major, and already she was beginning to see how rigorous it might be if she were to continue on to medical school. Her classes were full of smart, chatty girls who had dreamed about being doctors since they were younger. She threw herself into her books and tried to keep up, but found college to be ten times harder than high school had ever been.

Luckily, Felicia was pre-med as well, so they huddled together for study sessions and helped each other learn everything they needed to know.

Tami was an English major and kept her head in her books, writing papers at midnight and regularly falling asleep with books in her bed. April was a political science major and equally as busy as everyone else.

It wasn't until late October that they all managed to get their schedules to sync up and spend a night out in the city together.

Nia was trying hard to keep her relationship with Patrice going, but it was hard.

She hadn't anticipated being so busy her freshman year and Patrice, who was adjusting to a completely different city and culture, was just as frazzled.

They managed to text each other a few times a week, but nothing too deep – just silly photos or stories on how they had goofed on campus. They were trying to make plans to do something together for winter break, but who knew how well that would work out.

Nia felt like she was adjusting well to college, managing to see her parents and PJ every couple of weeks and handling her responsibilities on her own. "I'm proud of you," her mom said. "You haven't asked me for money once!" Nia didn't want to burst her bubble and tell her it was because she had been asking her dad, so she let the compliment slide.

Every once in a while, if she slowed down a bit, she thought about Brandon. They hadn't spoken much since graduation and Nia realized that they were growing apart. He would text her from time to time, but they were just brief "what you doing" messages, so she'd take a day or two to respond on purpose. Slowly she could see he would be fading to black soon.

She decided to just focus on school and let that be enough on her plate. There was no shortage of cute guys in Atlanta. *When the time is right*, she thought, *I'll find someone worth spending time with.*

Mya, on the other hand, did not share the same philosophy. They usually hung out on Thursdays, the one day they both had a pocket of free time in the afternoon. One Thursday in early November, they went off campus to Soul Vegetarian, a vegan restaurant. Mya had recently given up meat and was obsessed with finding new places she could eat. Nia thought Mya was lucky that she was one of her best friends, because there weren't too many people she'd let convince her to trade chicken wings and fries for green smoothies and lentil burgers.

"You young girls got it all wrong," Mya said, slurping up the rest of her smoothie. "How old are you, by the way?"

Nia laughed. "You don't know how old I am?"

"Nope. You're... eighteen? nineteen?" Mya skimmed her from head to toe. "You look about sixteen, if I had to guess."

"Whatever! I'm eighteen."

"Ha!" Mya slapped her hand on the table. "You're a baby." Nia already knew how old Mya was, of course — her friend was turning 21 in a few weeks and spent every day giving her friends a countdown. This morning's text, three weeks out, simply said: *21 'til 21!*

"So what is it that I'm not understanding?"

"That this is the perfect time to find a husband," Mya said, excitedly. "You see, I've been working on this hypothesis for a while now and it makes perfect sense. We walk by smart, eligible men all day, every day here. We're right next to Morehouse and Clark Atlanta—they are full of our future husbands! That's why we gotta keep our eyes open *now,* while we're close enough to touch 'em. Before they scatter to all ends of the country."

Nia raised an eyebrow but sipped her drink and played along with her friend. "So how is your husband hunt going?"

Mya smiled widely. "Great. I've got three dates this week."

"Three?" Nia almost choked on her smoothie. "How did you get three dates? In the same week?"

"Well, Jordan goes to my church and he's been trying to take me out for a while, so I figured I'd see how that goes. Malcolm lives in the building next door —he helped me with my bags a few weeks back and we've been talking ever since. And Shawn? Well, he's just a cutie so I *had* to say yes when he asked me out."

Nia raised an eyebrow.

"What?" Mya said, setting down her glass. "It's not like I'm sleeping with any of them. I don't get down like that. I just like to spend time getting to know them and letting them get to know me."

She pulled a book out of her bag and slid it across the table to Nia. "Have you read this?"

Nia held it up. Smiling up from the cover was a black couple, Devon Franklin and Meagan Good, snuggled in a warm embrace. Under their picture was the title *The Wait: A Powerful Practice for Finding the Love of Your Life and the Life You Love.*

"I think I heard about this book," Nia said, flipping it to the back cover.

"I read it last weekend. It's so good! You can have that copy if you want."

"What's it about?" Nia said, flipping through some of the pages. "Just a hundred pages telling folks not to have sex?"

"No!" Mya said, laughing. "It's about *more* than sex. It's about figuring out how to have a great relationship, without things getting messy or complicated. That's why I'm able to date three guys at once—because I'm not interested in a sexual relationship. I just want to have fun with a guy who makes me laugh and respects me. And once a certain someone makes it known that he's husband potential, then the other fellas gotta go bye-bye."

Nia just nodded and took it all in. "So basically you're just having fun?"

"Right!" Mya leaned in close. "You can't go too fast with these guys, Nia. You gotta make them put in their time, show you who they really are. That way you weed out the crazy ones, the dangerous ones, the broken ones ..."

"The dumb ones!" Nia blurted out. The two of them laughed so hard the other customers turned to stare.

"But seriously," Mya said, tapping the cover of the book. "I believe what they're saying. Sex makes you go all goo-goo eyed over somebody and you get caught up! You take sex off the table, and it makes everything so much easier."

"Okay, I'll read it." Nia slipped it into her bag.

"So who are you dating these days?"

"Nobody," Nia said, laughing. "I'm single as they come."

"There's *nobody* you got your eye on?"

"I'm focused on school," Nia replied. "Being a bio major ain't no joke!"

"Yeah, that's true. I'm surprised you even had time to come out today."

"I know." Nia picked at the rest of her salad. "It's not like I'd have time to date somebody even if I wanted to. I'm studying about four hours a day now."

"What about that one boy that you used to talk to in high school? Brandon?"

"Oh, that's over," Nia said with a wave of her hand. "He didn't want to wait so…here I am. Single and free."

"Good for you," Mya said. She covered Nia's hand with her own. "Really, girl. That is really hard to do. I'm proud of you."

"Thanks." She pulled out her phone to check the time. "Ugh, I gotta meet Felicia at the library in twenty minutes."

"Need me to drop you off?"

"Could you?"

"Yeah, I've got time. Anything for my lil' sis." She winked at Nia and scooped up their trash. The two of them headed to the exit, still chatting about the upcoming weekend.

***

Two hours later, Felicia closed her book and stretched. "Girl, what were we thinking?"

Nia yawned. "I have no idea. I could really sleep for a week at this point."

They collected their books and headed for the library exit. The fall air was cool and the temperature was dropping rapidly. Nia shivered. "This cold air is making me even more tired."

"Right? I'm about to go back to Abby and be knocked out," Felicia joked. "I'm gonna be snoring so loud tonight. Poor April."

"How is April doing? I haven't seen her in like two weeks."

"She's good," Felicia said slowly. "I think she might transfer though."

"Transfer? Why?"

"Because she misses being on a team. She gave up some nice scholarship offers to come here because she didn't want to disappoint her parents, but I think she's regretting it a little."

Nia was stunned. She didn't realize her friend had even been thinking about leaving. The college didn't have a true athletic program, but Nia had been so wrapped up in her own life that she hadn't even considered how difficult the decision to come here anyway must have been for April. "I think I'll come back to Abby with you and see if April's there. We should all talk with her."

Felicia nodded. "Sounds good. But don't think I'm rude if I fall asleep in the middle of the conversation."

"Okay, I won't," Nia promised.

***

"Guys, I'm fine," April insisted. She was sitting on her bed with a pile of clothes fresh from the dryer between her legs. "It's not a big deal."

"That's not what you told me on Monday," Felicia reminded her.

"It's just that..." April stopped folding and pushed the clothes to the side. "The basketball season is starting soon and I've been looking at all the photos of my friends at practice and I do miss it. I didn't realize how hard it would be."

"You're thinking about leaving?" Nia asked. She wanted to cut to the chase.

"I don't know," April said. "I know my mom was so happy to have me here, and I do enjoy being here with you guys. Classes are great, and the people are great. But...I play ball. That's what I do. I love it."

Nia and Felicia got quiet for a moment. Then Felicia broke the silence.

"So maybe you should talk to your parents." she suggested. "Tell them what you told us."

"I don't think you guys know my parents," April said, frustrated. "They would rather I come here, where I only have a handful of scholarships versus going someplace where I was offered a full ride. Spelman means that much to them."

"But what about you?" Nia urged.

"I guess I'm happy here."

"Nah, girl, I know you better than that. Call your mom. Talk to her."

"You think that's a good idea?"

"Yes," Nia and Felicia said in unison.

"Okay," April said. "I'll call her tonight."

"Good," Nia said. "Because it's no sense in denying that you are definitely meant to be playing ball somewhere. I remember you were a beast on the court."

"I want to see you play," Felicia said, nudging her friend on the shoulder.

"So we have to make that happen."

April smiled. "Y'all are good people," she said. "Thanks for looking out for me."

"Anytime," Nia replied. She slung her bag over her head and headed for the door."

"After you call your mom, call me and let me know how it went, okay?"

"Will do."

***

The following Thursday, Mya had invited Nia over to meet her roommates, as Nia had been at Spelman for over two months, and Mya was tired of feeling like she still lived on campus. The plan was to snack and chill for a couple hours, until Nia had to meet her study group later that evening.

"This is Camille," Mya said, gesturing to her roommate. "She's bougie so I don't pay her any attention. Camille, this is Nia."

"Whatever," Camille said, smiling and hugging Nia close.

Mya looked around the apartment. "Is Kelli here?"

"Nope, she went over to her boyfriend's place," Camille said, walking over to the couch and grabbing the remote. She flipped to HGTV and sat, mesmerized at the house renovations and projects.

"She does this all day," Mya said, rolling her eyes. "This is why I called her bougie."

"I can't wait to get a house," Camille said, ignoring Mya's comment. "I don't mind living here with you, girl, but whew, renting is so expensive."

"We're going to need another roommate in a minute if the rent keeps going up. She's gonna have to sleep in the kitchen."

"And get another to sleep over there in the corner," Camille said, gesturing behind the sofa. Mya recognized a slight lift at the end of all of Camille's words and wondered where her accent came from.

Nia sat down on the couch next to Camille and curled up to watch the rest of the show. "Where are you from originally?" Nia asked.

"St. Croix," she said. "My family moved here in the ninth grade, but both of my parents went to college in the states."

Mya poked her head in the room from the kitchen. "You want some of this kale juice?"

Nia screwed up her face. "Eh, no thank you. You have any coke?"

"And she calls *me* bougie! She's the one drinking kale juice!" Camille cackled.

"I'm just trying to be healthy." Mya laughed, handing Nia a coke and settling down on the rug with her kale juice. "I'll have you know since I started drinking this stuff all my acne went away. It's like magic juice."

"I'll have to take your word for it," Nia said, sipping her coke.

The three of them heard keys jingling in the doorway. "Kelli's back," Mya said, scooting to the side so Kelli could have a clear path into the apartment.

A few seconds later, Kelli opened the door, her cheeks red from the wind outside. Her hair was tousled a bit, curls all over her head.

"Did the wind do that or is that because of Anthony?" Mya teased.

"Don't be teasing me in front of company," Kelli said, pulling off her jacket and looking directly at Nia. "She's going to get the wrong idea about me."

Kelli had a strong Brooklyn accent, and Nia could tell she was the type of girl who didn't hesitate to speak her mind.

"This is Nia," Camille said, gesturing to her without taking her eyes off the TV.

"You know, Mya's lil' sis?"

"Oh yeah," Kelli said. "How you doing?"

"I'm good," Nia said, suddenly feeling like she was about thirteen years old. When Kelli spoke and moved, there was no doubt a woman was in the room.

Nia was still trying to feel like a woman, but most times she felt like she came up short.

Kelli got settled on the floor opposite Mya. Nia curled up on the couch.

Mya used the opportunity to do her yoga stretches, while Kelli leaned back and closed her eyes, apparently tired from whatever she had done at Anthony's place.

The four of them watched TV, ate and made fun of Mya's healthy snacks. They laughed about some of the antics they'd witnessed on the quad. Before Nia knew it, it was time for her to head to study group. She was enjoying just getting some rest and hanging out, and didn't feel like interrupting it to go study, but she didn't want to chance falling behind.

"I'll see you all later," Nia said, gathering her belongings and heading to the door. "Y'all pray for my strength. This semester is killing me."

"You got this! Just think about all those nice doctor checks you'll be getting," Mya said. She gave Nia a salute and Nia headed back to the local train station, for a long night of studying at the dorm.

Let's Talk – First year of college

There is a vast difference between high school and college. In high school, you're still part of a collective. The teachers view you as a group, and there is protection to keep you from falling too far behind—parent-teacher conferences, progress reports, detention.

In college, it's sink or swim. There are no professors chasing behind you, your parents don't automatically get access to your grades (even if they're paying), and there's no one to wake you up in the morning but you. It's you, on your own, making your own decisions. It can be scary to think about how suddenly the responsibilities shift, but many people have gone to college before you and survived one way or another.

So how can you succeed in this new environment? These are my best tips:

Get a Good Crew

Nia's transition to college is eased by the fact that she has a great group of girlfriends to help motivate her when she's stressed about classes, and party with her when she's ready to have a little fun. Good friends are the ones who challenge you and look out for you. The great thing about college is that, for most of you, your core group of high school friends is gone, so you're all looking for new people to hang out with and develop real, genuine relationships. These friendships can be your lifeline during difficult semesters and a source of strength when you may question, *What am I doing here?*

So how do you find new friends? Don't be afraid to just walk the halls in your dorm and say hello to dorm mates, knock on the door and invite them to hang out with you. If you're living off-campus, spend a little time walking around campus after classes. Don't just rush home.

Find one or two people in your classes that you can get to know a little better and maybe form a study group to help you excel in the classroom.

You can look at local "meetup" meetings to find people who are interested in the same things you are. Remember that people need people; you can't be an island.

While the goal is to develop new friendships, be aware that some friendships can be toxic – those relationships where people are only around you because of what they can get from you.

Real friendships are built on give and take.

Keep an eye out for relationships that only exist because you're the one who has a car or because you know someone on the football team.

On the flip side, your friendships from high school don't have to die. You might be entering a new phase where you, like Nia, are trying to figure out what womanhood looks like.

It can be comforting to have friends who understand who you are and you have a shared history with.

Get in the Habit of Excellence

The biggest mistake I see students make is thinking they can coast their freshman year. In reality, you will build on everything you learn your first year, so it's in your best interest to knock it out of the park for the first few semesters. It's a lot easier to begin with a high GPA and run into a few hard classes later on, than it is to start with a low GPA and try to raise it.

Also, don't miss classes if you can help it. It's tempting to skip classes to sleep in or goof off (especially since many professors don't take attendance) but in the long run, you'll only be hurting yourself. You're putting money toward this education (whether you're paying out of pocket or using loans, which you will have to pay back later) so get up and go to class. Not going is the equivalent of buying a car and just letting it sit in the driveway — put your classes to use!

Get organized at the beginning of every semester. Your professors will usually hand out a syllabus, which details everything you need to know for the course—textbooks, test dates, assignments and attendance policy. Make sure you remember those dates by putting them in your calendar, whether online or a physical planner. (Also plug in reminders about a week before any big assignment so you don't catch yourself doing last minute work!)

Studying in college is much different from studying in high school, so take the time to discover the best study set-up for you. Are you the type who needs music or background noise, or complete silence? Do you like to sit at a desk or move around? Do you like to be alone or with a partner? Find out what helps you retain the information so you can excel.

Get Out of the Room

Along with making new friends, it's good to spend time getting out of your dorm room. It's tempting to sit in your room (you pay enough for it!) by yourself, but it's important to get out and see what's happening. Scope out bulletin boards, sit on the quad and see what flyers are circulating. Go to on-campus events, movie nights and house parties. Study in the library. Hang out in the common areas of the hall. Make yourself visible so good opportunities and friendships can come your way.

Get Involved

Sure, you're at college to learn but you're also there to develop crucial skills that can't be discovered in the classroom. Most colleges have a decent sized office of student life, with on-campus organizations covering everything from campus politics to Greek life. Find something that interests you and get involved. This is also one of the best ways to meet new people.

Retain Your Spiritual Center

During your college years you may have experiences that test your faith, so it's important for you to stay connected to what gives you strength. Most colleges have an on-campus chapel, nearby churches and organizations that can connect you to a variety of faith-based services, whatever your beliefs.

Chapter Eight: Plus 1

"Breathe in; hold your breath for seven seconds, then release." The yoga instructor walked around the room, gently pushing shoulders down and realigning hips as Mya and Nia tried to relax in their first yoga class. Students get to take them for free at the wellness center, and Nia was trying to squeeze every last benefit out of all this tuition she was paying.

"Let's go into corpse pose, hold that for ten seconds...let your body sink into the floor, feel your head, shoulders, belly, thighs, feet all sink into the floor."

Nia usually had a hard time relaxing fully, but the instructor's calm, relaxing voice almost put Nia to sleep.

Once class was over, they rolled up their mats, said goodbye to the instructor and walked back to Mya's apartment, where Nia had been staying while Tami's boyfriend was visiting from out of town.

"I feel so relaxed," Nia said, feeling the tension gone in her shoulders and lower back. "I always thought yoga was boring, but I feel like I just had a massage."

"Same," Mya said, gripping her arm with the opposite hand and pulling it toward her for a stretch. "That was almost better than a massage. I'm going back tomorrow."

Nia and Mya returned to Mya's apartment to find Camille crying in the bathroom.

"Camille, what's wrong?" Mya said, rushing in and kneeling next to Camille by the tub.

Camille didn't respond, but simply nodded toward the sink. Mya looked up and saw a pregnancy test balanced on the side. She didn't have to look at it to know what was causing the tears.

"I'm pregnant," Camille whispered. "I can't believe it. I'm only twenty. What am I going to do with a baby?"

Nia felt weird still standing in the doorway, so even though she wasn't that close to Camille, she figured it was better to offer her some comfort than to hover around. She sat on the other side of Camille and rubbed her shoulders. "You'll figure it out."

Camille shook her head. "Having a baby is not in my plans right now."

"Are you going to tell Davis?" Mya asked quietly. Davis was Camille's boyfriend of two years, the guy she had locked eyes on at homecoming freshman year and just never let go of.

"I already sent him a text," she sniffled.

"What did he say?"

"That I should come over. But I'm not in the mood to talk right now."

The three of them sat there for a while, not sure what to say to comfort their friend. "You want something to drink?" Mya offered.

Camille nodded and Mya went into the kitchen. A few seconds later she reappeared with a bottle of Gatorade. "Drink this," she urged, rubbing Camille's back as she took a sip. "You feel a little better?"

"Yeah," Camille said, slowly. "It's...just a shock."

"I bet," Mya agreed. "Do you want to be alone right now? We can give you some privacy if you'd like?"

"Yeah, I think I'm going to head to bed now." Camille heaved herself off the floor and wiped her eyes. "I'll be fine. I just need to sleep for a little bit and figure out what I'm going to do."

Mya and Nia nodded silently as Camille left.

"Wow," Mya said, picking up the pregnancy test and staring at it for a minute. "I can't believe she's about to be a mom."

"Well, she might not keep it," Nia offered, sitting up on the side of the tub.

"No, I know Camille," Mya insisted. "She's probably going to have this baby."

"You sure? She seemed pretty upset."

"Yeah, I'm sure. She's going to go to sleep tonight and then wake up in the morning with a plan. Camille always has a plan."

***

In her second semester of freshman year, Nia was in line at the bookstore when she thought she saw a woman who looked a bit like Camille from behind. She peered over the shoulder of the people in front of her and instantly spotted Camille's rounded belly as she turned to leave.

Nia hopped out of line and went up to Camille to hug her. "How are you doing?" Nia asked.

Camille smiled weakly. "I'm alright. Just getting over this morning sickness. It's been all day long so far. But I'm four months along so now I can at least keep food down."

"Well, you look good, girl," Nia said. "You don't look like you've been sick."

She pushed her braids out of her face. "Thank God for that." She nodded to the door. "Walk with me?"

The two of them left the bookstore and headed a short way off campus to catch the train, to Mya and Camille's apartment. Camille put her hands on her belly and turned toward Nia as they walked. "So I don't know if Mya told you, but I've decided that I'm probably going to sit out first semester senior year."

"Really?"

"Yeah, my due date is August 15, which is too close to the beginning of the semester. If I'm going to do this, I want to do this right, so I want to have some time with my little guy."

"It's a boy?" Nia exclaimed.

"Yup, a little boy." For the first time, Camille looked genuinely excited. "Found out on Tuesday. Davis is so happy."

"That's so great," Nia said, reaching out to squeeze her. "I mean, if it was a girl, that'd be great too. It's just that you're having a boy so..."

"Girl, I get it. I tell people I'm having a boy and they get all excited because they *know*. And I'm glad I know now. Makes it easier for me to envision being a mom."

"And how is Davis acting? Excited to be a dad?"

Camille scoffed. "Girl, he's so annoying now. It's like he doesn't understand what it means to be pregnant. He expects me to still have energy and not have morning sickness and not just feel tired all the time."

"Aw, I'm sorry."

"Not your fault," Camille said with a wave of her hand. "We're working it out but yeah, a baby changes everything. And he's not even here yet!"

They reached Camille's apartment and Nia gave Camille a big hug and bent down to talk to Camille's belly. "You be good in there for your mom. No more making her sick, alright?"

"Oh, I hope he listens to you. God, I hope he listens." Camille laughed. "Thanks for walking with me. I always feel so weird when I'm by myself on campus ever since I started showing. It's like people look at me differently now."

"No, I don't think they are," Nia lied. She wanted to reassure Camille, but she saw the looks from other students on the short walk from the bookstore. They were definitely staring and Nia had hoped Camille hadn't noticed.

"You don't have to lie. I have eyes. I can see it." She took a deep breath.

"But soon my little guy will be here and they'll have something else to stare at."

"So you probably won't come back until the spring?" Nia asked.

"That's what it's looking like. I have so much stuff to get ready by August—need to save money, find a new apartment..."

"You're moving?" Nia was surprised.

"Yeah, girl. I can't live here with two roommates and a baby. They didn't sign up for that. Plus, this place is expensive. I was barely making my portion of the rent before the baby. Now it's too much for me to pay with little man coming. So I'm gonna move and try to get a cheaper place."

Nia didn't want to say it, but with moving and sitting out a semester, it seemed like everything in Camille's life was changing. *Was this how her mom felt all those years ago?*

"Well, if you need anything, just let me know," Nia offered. "I could maybe babysit for a couple hours while you study?"

"I would really appreciate that," Camille said. She dug her keys out of her purse. "Well, I gotta go inside so I can find something to eat. I'll talk to you later."

"Talk to you later." Nia waved and turned back down the street to head back to campus.

***

One week later, Nia and April were walking across campus to check out this new student organization, Christians With Purpose. They called themselves CWP, for short, and they were all about being "realistic Christians." Mya was a member. She had invited Nia and April a few times before but their schedules never really worked out. Now they had a Wednesday evening free so they were trekking down to the student center atrium, mostly because Mya said there was free pizza and drinks. "I hope it's not veggie pizza," April said as they jogged up the steps to the hall.

"Knowing Mya, it probably is," Nia joked.

Sure enough, once they found the room for the meeting, there were three pizzas left, one spinach and mushroom and the other two were some sort of pepper and onion mix—luckily someone had asked for pepperoni also. Mya waved to them from the corner of the room where she was munching on a slice and signaled to her friends in the group that she wanted to introduce them.

"I'm glad you made it," Mya said, hugging the two of them, smelling just like the slice of pizza in her hand.

The two of them tried not to stare too hard at the pizza, as it had been hours since they last ate. "Of course. We wanted to see what this was all about," April said.

Mya nodded to the two young women behind her. "Guys, this is Kendra," she said, motioning to the taller one with blond streaks, "and this is Eboni." Eboni had a cute mini fro that instantly made Nia think she was a very confident woman. *Anyone who rocked her hair that short had to be*, she thought to herself.

"Welcome to the group," Eboni said. She gestured to the table. "Go ahead and get some pizza. We'll be starting in a few minutes."

The two of them huddled quietly in the corner with their pizza slices—Nia tried the spinach pizza, which surprisingly wasn't that bad, and April had the pepperoni. As soon as they got up to toss their paper plates away, Eboni stood up to call the meeting to order.

"I'm glad you all could make it tonight," Eboni said. "I know it's a little chilly outside so I'm glad you took the time to come meet with us. I think we're going to have a great discussion tonight."

She motioned for everyone to gather around in a circle. The ten or so members assembled quickly. "Cell phones off," she reminded the group.

"Cell phones off?" April muttered. "Like, off-off?"

"Yes," Mya said. "We like to make sure we are focusing on one thing.

It can be distracting if your phone goes off or keeps buzzing."

Nia and April looked at each other and then slid their phones to silent.

"Now then," Eboni said, clasping her hands in front of her. "Let's welcome Nia and April to the meeting – we're so happy they could join us." Everyone turned to the two of them and gave them a quick head nod. Nia gave a shy nod back, while April said, "Hey everyone! Happy to be here and see what this is all about."

"Well, our meetings tend to be really informal," Eboni said, leaning back against the chair. "We discuss upcoming business and then we just talk. What's first on the agenda, Kendra?"

"Our upcoming 'Let's Talk About Sex' event is in two weeks," Kendra said, reading from a folded piece of paper. "It's going to be from 7 to 9 and we're just about done getting the speakers and food. Dana is getting flyers and Michelle will be taking notes."

Nia and April exchanged a glance that said, *A sex event? What kind of Christian organization was this?*

Mya caught the look on their faces and laughed. "Yes, we talk about everything here. We think it's so important for women our age to talk about sex and what it's really supposed to be."

"Yes," Kendra said. "We host our Let's Talk About Sex event every March, and it's one of the biggest events on campus every year."

Nia raised an eyebrow but didn't say anything. April, of course, had a question.

"So, um, what exactly do y'all talk about at this event? Because it doesn't take two hours to tell folks, 'Just wait.' Isn't that what you're going to be doing?"

"We do talk about waiting," Eboni agreed. "But we also talk about the realities of sex. We know that not everyone is waiting, so we talk about birth control, STDs..."

"Sounds...fun," April said dryly. Nia nudged her to hush.

"It *is* fun," Eboni said. "You'll see. Will you come join us?"

"We'll be there," Nia interrupted, begging April with her eyes to stop embarrassing her.

April laughed at her friend and nodded toward Eboni. "Yeah, we'll be there."

Eboni smiled. "Great. I think you'll both enjoy the program."

***

"I'm not sure about this," April said as they began the trek back to the dorms. "You know I love you and your virginity pledge or whatever you call it, but I have needs."

"It's not a virginity pledge," Nia said, poking her friend in the ribs. "It's just...I'm waiting for the right guy."

"Girl, there are plenty of 'right guys' over there," she said, jerking her head in the direction of Morehouse.

"I'm for real," Nia said. "I've seen too much—starting with my own mother."

"You're still on that? You gotta let that go. Your mom did just fine with you and PJ."

"Yeah, but we threw her off course so much. Oh, and Camille!"

"Who?" April said, pulling her chapstick out of her pocket.

"I keep forgetting you don't know her. Mya's roommate?"

"Oh, yeah. You've mentioned her before, I think."

"Yes, she's pregnant. About four months along."

"Oh wow."

"Yes. I saw her today and she's talking about how she's going to sit out a semester or two once the baby's born."

April scrunched up her face. "Why she gotta do that?"

"Because she's due in August and it's too close to the start of school. Plus, she has to move so she's got a lot to do before her son gets here."

"Why does she have to move?" April said, scrunching up her face again.

"Because she's having a baby," Nia explained patiently. "You want Felicia to bring her crying baby home to where you live?"

"I'm a good friend," April said, shrugging.

"Well, Camille can't afford their apartment anymore with the baby coming. Hopefully she'll be able to find someplace with her boyfriend and they can live together, save some money."

"So Camille is why you don't want to have sex?"

"Not just Camille. Remember Patrice and Marcus?"

April nodded. "Yeah, that had me shook for a while too."

"See, exactly! I just don't feel like I can trust these guys out here. It feels like everything falls on us —*we're* the ones who get pregnant, if we get some type of STD, *we're* the ones who get all messed up and then we can't have kids. We're the ones who have to miss a semester of school while the guy gets to live his life like everything's fine."

"Hey, you don't have to justify your reasons to me," April said, throwing her hands up.

"I'm just saying —I'm trying to be a doctor. You know how many nights I have fallen asleep at the library and the staff had to wake me and tell me to go home? I can't throw away all the hard work I've put in so far just for any ol' guy. Nope. He's got to be special."

"And how can you tell the guy is special?"

"Well, Mya gave me this book," Nia turned and pulled her copy of *The Wait* out of her bag. "It says that when you don't have sex with a guy, it's easier for you to tell if he's got potential. You're not all caught up and making excuses for his behavior."

"And you want *me* to read this?" April joked, flipping the book to the back cover. "What you trying to say?"

"You don't have to read it," Nia said. "Besides, I know if I let you borrow it I'll never see it again."

"True." April laughed.

They arrived at Nia's dorm and Nia hugged her friend goodbye. "See you tomorrow?"

"Yup," April said. "See you tomorrow."

Let's Talk — Birth control

College is a whole new ballgame when it comes to sex, relationships and your future.

Here, you are not under the watchful eye of your parents (unless you still live at home).

Now the decisions you make are truly your own, and they can have a ripple effect for years down the line.

Let's talk about Camille for a moment. She is a bright student who is now racing against the clock to get ready for the arrival of her first child. She didn't plan on having a child at this point, but she's decided to become a mom. Before the child even gets here, though, there are multiple sacrifices she has to make: finding a new place to live, having her relationship tested, and sitting out a semester. It's probably safe to say that she didn't think one night of sex would lead to an upheaval in her world.

Unplanned pregnancy is one of the biggest challenges you can face as a young woman. It can be hard to work your way through school even without a child. Becoming a parent means that you have another person to think about in every decision you make. Like Camille, you may find that you won't be able to progress through college like you envisioned or that it'll take you longer to create the life you want for yourself.

Let me also take a moment to reiterate something — for the most part, young women like you are very fertile. It's not as hard as you think to get pregnant, and we want to delay that moment until you feel you are ready for the responsibility — financially and emotionally.

Let's run down the various birth control options on the market. Many insurance plans cover birth control for the cost of your co-pay. If you're still on your parents' insurance, see what the plan covers and how much you can be expected to pay out of pocket:

Birth Control pills

How does it work? The pill might be one of the first birth control methods you were familiar with, due to its popularity in our culture. Users have to take a pill every day of the month, same time of day. It works by preventing your ovaries from releasing eggs. Some brands also keep sperm from reaching the eggs by thickening your cervical mucus. Some women are prescribed birth control pills to help other health problems such as acne or painful periods. The pill doesn't protect against STDs, so I recommend a condom with this method.

Effectiveness: 91%

Side effects: Sore breasts, nausea, spotting, and decreased sex drive.

The IUD

How does it work? The IUD is a small, plastic T-shaped device that sits inside your uterus. IUDs work as sort of "sperm scarecrows." They keep sperm from reaching the eggs by making your cervical mucus thicker and interfering with the way sperm move. There are two types of IUDs — hormonal and non-hormonal. Of the hormonal variety, there are three options, each application lasting anywhere from three to six years. The non-hormonal version lasts up to 12 years.

IUDs are inserted during a regular doctor visit. Having it removed will take place in a doctor's office as well. The biggest benefit of an IUD is that once it's inserted, there's nothing else for you to do to be protected against pregnancy. (I still strongly recommend the use of condoms as the IUD does not protect against STDs.)

Effectiveness: 99%

Side Effects: Bleeding between periods, increased period bleeding (for the non-hormonal IUD users), ovarian cysts, cramps.

Implants

How does it work? A thin matchstick-sized rod gets inserted under your skin in a doctor's office, protecting you from pregnancy for up to four years. It releases hormones that prevent your ovaries from releasing eggs.

The implant will also thicken your cervical mucus, which helps to block sperm from getting to the egg in the first place.

Effectiveness: 99%

Side Effects: Irregular bleeding (particularly for the first year), acne, change in appetite.

The Shot

How does it work? Every three months you go to the doctor for a shot of progestin, which like the IUD, keeps sperm from reaching the eggs by thickening your cervical mucus. It also prevents your ovaries from releasing eggs. It is a very effective method, providing you keep the regular schedule of shots with your doctor. It's also a relatively private method—there's nothing for you to do or nothing you need to keep with you in order to be protected from pregnancy. But none of these methods protect you from STDs, so I always recommend using a condom as a secondary measure of protection.

Effectiveness: 94%

Side Effects: Irregular bleeding, weight gain, tender breasts, headache.

Diaphragm

How does it work? It's a thin silicone dome that covers your cervix and prevents sperm from reaching the egg. It is often used in combination with spermicide, a cream or foam that keeps sperm from moving. (Spermicide can also be used on its own, but it is most often recommended to be used with a barrier method for most effectiveness.)

Effectiveness: 88%

Side Effects: Vaginal irritation, frequent urinary tract infections, difficulty inserting.

Condoms

How does it work? Condoms are one of the most popular forms of birth control and for good reasons – it is the only method that protects against pregnancy and STDs, it's cheap, and it's accessible. They work by allowing the man to ejaculate into the thin latex instead of into the woman's vagina. They are easy to put on in the heat of the moment by either person (man or woman). They come in all types of varieties and sizes.

Effectiveness: 82%

Side Effects: Allergic reaction, irritation to lubricant.

The Patch

How does it work? The patch looks like a big, square Band-Aid. You apply one patch on your butt, stomach, upper outer arm, or upper torso (however not on your breasts) for three weeks, changing it weekly. In the fourth week, you go patch-free. It works like a lot of other methods, by giving off hormones that prevent your ovaries from releasing eggs and thickening your cervical mucus to block sperm.

Effectiveness: 91%

Side Effects: Irritation at the application site, nausea, irregular bleeding, sore breasts.

The Ring

How does it work? The ring is a soft plastic ring that goes into your vagina for three weeks at a time. On the fourth week, you take it out. It works by releasing a hormone that stops your ovaries from releasing an egg, and it also thickens your cervical mucus so that sperm can't reach any eggs anyway. You insert the ring yourself, so it is a good method for women who are comfortable with their bodies. I also recommend using a condom with this method, as the ring does not protect against STDs.

Effectiveness: 91%

Side Effects: Bleeding in between periods, tender breasts, nausea and vomiting.

Withdrawal

How does it work? I hesitate to even include this here, but it is one of the oldest and most widely used "methods" of birth control. The majority of sexually active adults have used this method at least once, so I feel obligated to include it. The withdrawal method is very simple —it means the man will "pull out" before he ejaculates, so that the sperm does not get deposited into the vagina, where it can then travel to meet the egg. I advise against this method for two reasons: one, most men cannot properly time their ejaculation for this method to be effective. And two, this method is about having sex without a condom, something I do not recommend outside of marriage. Withdrawal might be a way to try to protect yourself from pregnancy, but it carries all the risks of sexually transmitted diseases.

Effectiveness: 78%

Side Effects: None, other than a higher risk of pregnancy.

In addition to the methods listed above, there is also something called emergency contraception, also known as the "morning-after pill." It's a pill you take up to five days after unprotected sex or in cases of sexual assault that will prevent a pregnancy from occurring. The sooner you take it, the more effective it can be. There are four versions on the market and the most widely known version, Plan B, is available without a prescription. It's not meant to be used as a regular method of birth control, hence the name, emergency contraception.

What You Should Know – Which birth control is right for me?

One great resource I recommend is Bedsider.org. The site has comprehensive information about all types of birth control, including videos from young people who share what their experience with each of the methods has been like. It has a comparison tool that allows you to view two or more methods side-by-side to see which one is for you. There is also a list of providers in your area who will be able to get you started.

Once you've picked out a method and talked to your doctor, Bedsider also has birth control reminder texts, which can help you if you've picked a method that requires some effort from you, like the pill, patch or ring (they also have an app). Here are a few questions I review with my patients to help them choose a method that will keep them protected:

· What are the potential side effects?
· Can you be realistic in terms of your responsibility; for example, will you remember to take something every day?
· How much will it cost?

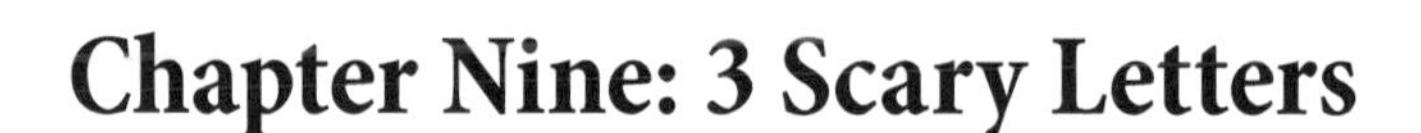

Chapter Nine: 3 Scary Letters

Felicia's voice cut through Nia's sleep. "Nia! Nia, girl, wake up!"

Nia groggily opened her eyes. "What is it? Who…?" She lifted her head off her textbook and looked around the room. "Oh my goodness, I think I fell asleep."

Felicia laughed. "You think? Girl, you were knocked out. You've got drool all over that textbook."

Nia didn't usually study in bed, but now that it was senior year, she felt this pressure to have her head in a book every waking minute. She had curled up in bed to do some reading, but her exhaustion levels were surely catching up with her. This wasn't the first time she accidentally used a book as a pillow.

Over the past three years, Nia had done remarkably well in school. She was acing most of her classes and getting help in those where she knew she could do better. She had maintained a 3.9 GPA while still being involved with a few student organizations.

So much had changed since freshman year. April had bowed out of following her family's footsteps and transferred to Georgia Tech, where she was now the starting guard for the Yellow Jackets. She was so happy now, and her friends were happy for her, packing the stands at her games and cheering for her louder than anyone else.

Patrice was blossoming at Howard and made it back to Atlanta every couple months to hang out and see her family. She was a political science major and had just completed an internship with the National Women's Law Center, where she was determined to work after graduation.

Nia and Tami kept in touch, but after Tami moved off campus sophomore year, they saw each other less and less. They still sent each other "hey girl" texts every couple weeks.

Nia had grown closer to Felicia through the years as they bonded over the rigors of their pre-med program. It seemed like any week that Nia was dragging and close to quitting was the week that Felicia had the most optimism and vice versa! They had to depend on and encourage each other to make it through, so they decided to live together senior year in one of the newer dorms.

Mya was still Mya, having graduated from Spelman two years prior. Nia had been worried about missing her friend, but they still managed to see each other at least once a month to hang out. Mya had since given up her vegan food, and Nia was so happy she could drag Mya to all the good soul food restaurants that they had avoided during her "no food with a face" phase. Nia was also very proud of her best friend. Mya had spent almost five years at Spelman working on her communications degree and now she worked at CNN, with hopes of working her way up to a producer's slot in the next few years.

Now it was Nia's turn to get ready to enter the real world. She was prepared, spending most of her waking moments thinking about medical school. She already had a good idea of what school she might attend, but her main goal was getting a good score on the MCAT, the admissions test for potential medical students. She felt like she was very well prepared, but all of her professors told her the same thing: "There's no such thing as being too prepared for this test." She took their advice to heart and set up a grueling study schedule, trying to prepare before she took the test in three months. Nia was nervous, but she knew that she wanted to be a doctor more than anything, so she was willing to put in the work to make her dreams a reality.

She stretched, lifting her arms to the sky and feeling tense in her neck and shoulders. She rubbed one side of her neck while reaching for her phone to check the time. "Crap, it's 7:30," she said, scrambling out of bed. "Why didn't you wake me up earlier?"

Felicia turned back to her desk, her piles of books and papers overflowing.

"Girl, you obviously needed that rest. Your body shut *down*."

"Yeah, but now I'm late to meet Maurice," she said, picking up clothes that were on the floor and tossing them onto the bed. When she got into hardcore study mode like this, she tended to turn into the world's biggest slob, which Felicia hated.

Nia grabbed a clean grey T-shirt from her drawer and slipped on some black leggings. "This will be like the third date I've been late to in the past three weeks. He's going to think I'm so rude."

Nia spritzed some water on her hair and fluffed it with her fingers. "Ugh, I should have twisted my hair last night. I knew better than to try to let it go one more day."

"Oh, stop it. Your hair is fine."

"And where are my shoes?" Nia got on all fours to look under her bed.

"They're not in the closet?" Felicia asked without looking around. Nia was constantly frazzled and was liable to put her shoes anywhere. Once, Felicia found them in the hallway.

"Here they are!" Nia exclaimed, pulling them from under a big pile of papers at the foot of her bed. She slipped them on and patted her pockets. "Now where are my keys?"

Felicia picked them up silently off her desk and handed them to Nia without taking her eyes off her textbook. "So where are you two going?"

"To the movies," Nia said, slipping her keys into her purse and grabbing her earrings off the dresser. "Some comedy. I don't know. I wasn't really paying attention when he told me."

Felicia laughed again. "You don't even sound like you're into him. So why are you going?"

"I *am* into him. I think."

"So he's just something to do?"

"No. I mean, he's someone to help me remember that life isn't just supposed to be about studying all the time. That even if I want to be a doctor, I also want to be a doctor with a life. I don't even remember what having fun is like. So yeah, I'm going to the movies with him."

"Remind me where he goes to school again? Morehouse?"

"Nope. Clark Atlanta."

"Ah, he's one of those." Felicia smirked. Ever since she'd broken up with her last boyfriend, a junior at CAU, Felicia kept insisting that all her friends needed to steer clear.

"He's not like Justin and you know it." Nia checked her phone again. *7:45*. She was supposed to meet him at 8 but that wasn't looking likely.

"Why didn't you just have him pick you up? Why do you always stress yourself out about meeting him somewhere?"

"Because I'm not trying to end up on the news," Nia explained. "You gotta really impress me before I'm thinking about going somewhere with you. The world is too crazy."

"You are so paranoid," Felicia said. She hugged Nia and waved her off. "Well, text me when you get there then."

Nia tried not to rush once she got in the car, remembering what her father always told her – *If you leave late, you'll arrive late.* So instead she took her time, stopping at yellow lights and trying to do the speed limit.

By the time she got to the theater, she was about 10 minutes late and Maurice was waiting by the concessions stand, already digging into the large popcorn in his arms.

"Sorry I'm late," she said weakly.

"It's okay. I'm starting to get used to it," he said, smiling at her. He leaned forward to kiss her cheek and all she could think was *He smells like butter.*

"You ready to go in?" Even though she was the one running late, Maurice was acting like they had all the time in the world. He hadn't moved from his spot since he'd spotted her, whereas Nia, who usually arrived ten minutes early everywhere, would have dragged him into the theater by now if he was the one who was late.

"After you," he said, sweeping his arm out in front of him.

They settled down into the seats and caught the last preview before the actual movie started. Nia had been wrong – this definitely wasn't a comedy, as the first ten minutes of the film featured two car chases and a shoot-out.

"I thought you said this was a funny movie?" she leaned over and whispered.

Maurice shook his head. "Nah, I said I had already seen that movie so we can see this one. You agreed. You don't remember?"

Nia didn't. She shrugged and leaned back in her seat. She was glad they had picked the theater where the seats reclined because she was still a little groggy from her nap.

Two hours later, Nia felt someone jostling her shoulder. "Nia, wake up."

She sat up, startled. "What happened?"

"You fell asleep," Maurice said with a smirk.

"I did?" She looked around the theater which was almost completely empty. A few workers had already swooped in with their brooms and dustpans to sweep up the snacks and cups that patrons had left on the floor.

"Yeah, come on, let's get out of here."

She followed Maurice silently, embarrassed that she had fallen asleep on a date. To be fair, she wasn't really interested in action movies, so the plot had bored her and the past two weeks she hadn't been getting more than five hours of sleep each night. She probably should have rescheduled. *Oh well.*

"Want to grab something to eat?" Maurice said, tossing his popcorn bag in the trash. "This place around the corner has great wings."

"I actually think I'm going to call it a night," Nia replied, yawning. "I'm really tired and I feel horrible for falling asleep on you in there. I don't want to make it twice and fall asleep during dinner too."

Maurice nodded. "That's okay. I know you have a lot going on right now."

"You want to do something Saturday?" Nia pulled out her phone to pull up her calendar.

"I can do Saturday," he said.

"No, actually, Saturday doesn't work. I have a practice test that day." She scrolled through her calendar again. "I have time on....Wednesday? Wait, no, that's a lab day. Hmm...how about next Friday?"

Maurice paused, waiting for her to change her mind about that date, which she did.

"Friday doesn't work either, Jesus. Okay um..." she looked up at him. "Maybe you should pull up your calendar too?"

He pulled his phone out but didn't move to check any dates, waiting for her to finally find a date that would work.

"Can you do the 25th? I have about three hours free in the afternoon?" she asked.

He looked at her and slowly put the phone back in his pocket.

"So you don't have a pocket of free time to see me until...three weeks from now?"

"I mean..." She scrolled through her calendar again. "No, not really. Not unless you want to study with me."

"What are you studying for? Midterms?"

"No, the MCAT."

"What's that?"

"The entrance exam that will help me get into medical school."

He nodded. "It sounds hard if it's got you studying like that."

"Yes, it's taking every little bit of my energy. That's why I fell asleep back there. I actually fell asleep while I was studying earlier and I only woke up because my roommate came back early from the library. I wasn't trying to be late today."

"Nah, it's cool," Maurice said. He shifted his weight a bit, like he was uncomfortable with her apology.

"I just want you to know I wasn't trying to be rude."

"I didn't think you were rude. I know you're a busy woman."

Nia closed her eyes and took a deep breath. "Listen, Maurice. I do like hanging out with you, but I'm not sure if this is going to work. Not right now anyway."

"I get it," he said, stuffing his hands in his pockets.

"I mean, I don't think it's fair to you. And I'm killing myself trying to remember stuff from class and my study sessions and...I don't think I should be dating right now. I can barely remember conversations we've had."

Maurice didn't say anything in response. Instead he simply hugged her and kissed her on the forehead. They stood still together for a moment and then he took a step back. "Good luck on the MCAT," he said. "Hope you get a great score."

"Thank you," she said, instantly regretting her decision. *Didn't I just say that my life couldn't be all about studying and medicine and that I needed to have a life outside the classroom?* Then she reminded herself of the mantra she used when she got overwhelmed with school: *This is all a temporary sacrifice.*

She got in the car and texted Felicia: *I fell asleep at the movies. SMH.*

Before she could put her seatbelt on, Felicia replied: *Girl what? How? Do we need to get you some vitamins?*

Nia laughed and typed out a quick reply: *It's a long story. Tell you when I get back.*

***

"Have you seen my headphones?" Nia asked Felicia, tearing up her desk to try to find the powder blue headphones her mom had splurged on and gotten her for Christmas. Nia was surprised to see them wrapped neatly on her bed when she came home for Christmas break. Her mom had obviously been listening when Nia complained that she needed music to study, and her earbuds kept slipping out of her ears.

"Um, check with Sam," Felicia said, nodding her head toward the room next door. "Didn't you let her borrow them?"

"Oh, that's right. She had that exam last week." Nia bounced up and headed over to Sam's room.

Sam was a bubbly junior who never ever stopped talking. Nia thought she was nice enough but she frequently had a headache whenever Sam left the room. She considered it might be the fact that Sam was one of the few white students at Spelman, and the only one in their hall, that made her so talkative and eager to fit in.

Sam answered the door on Nia's second knock. "Hey girl, what's up? You want to come in?

I got some pizza if you're hungry. You like pepperoni?"

"Hey," Nia said, fighting the urge to get straight to the point after she realized that she hadn't had much to eat that day besides a handful of popcorn and some Gatorade.

"Okay, I'll have a slice."

Sam waved her in and gestured to the table, where two paper plates were already laid out, like she knew Nia was going to come over.

"Patrick is on his way over," Sam said, catching on to Nia's confusion. "He won't mind though if you have some." Patrick must have been one of Sam's many boyfriends, a different one rotating through the halls practically every week.

A few months ago, Nia and Felicia had spotted Sam out at a downtown bar where she had obviously had too much to drink so they decided to take her home rather than leave her there to fend for herself. Drunk and loud in the back seat, she started rattling off the names of the guys she had slept with in the past year and why she dumped them. "David is a loser. Kevin smoked too much. Derrick, too short. Greg, too dumb…." Felicia rolled her eyes and tried to get her to hush. They'd heard rumors about how Sam would run through guys like water, but it was different to hear it coming from her own mouth. Nia had just sighed and tried to concentrate on driving.

Now Nia just chewed on her pizza and looked around the room. "Do you still have my headphones?" she asked, nibbling on the crust.

"Oh, I let Patrick borrow them," she said cheerfully. "He's bringing them over though so if you wait for him, I can give them to you."

You let some random dude borrow my expensive headphones? Nia thought to herself. "Who's Patrick?" she asked.

"He's this guy I'm seeing. Met him last week at the club. He's cool. He'll bring 'em by."

"Well, when I told you that you could borrow them, I meant that *you* could borrow them. Not Patrick."

The smile disappeared from Sam's face. "Oh, I didn't think you would mind."

Since she had been at Spelman, Nia had learned the best way to communicate was directly and honestly. "I do mind."

"I'm sorry. He just wanted to go for a run last time he was here so I let him borrow them but I guess he forgot to give them back so…."

Nia held up her hand to stop Sam's groveling. "Well, I gotta get back to studying. Just bring them by once you're done….doing whatever it is you all are getting ready to do. Why don't you text him to make sure he remembers to bring them."

Nia tossed her paper plate in the trash and gave a small half-wave to Sam. "I'll see you later?"

"See you later," she said, cheerfully. "I'll bring them by as soon as he gets here."

***

Two weeks later, Nia was surprised to see Sam standing outside her door.

"What's wrong?"

Sam looked distressed, and she kept tugging on her hair and twisting it around her fingers, something Nia recognized as a nervous tic.

"I went to the doctor two weeks ago to get tested like I always do. Now the doctor wants me to come in this afternoon so he can go over my results with me in person. He sounded weird on the phone, like I need to brace myself for bad news."

"I'm sure it's fine," Nia said, rubbing Sam's shoulder. "It's probably nothing."

"I don't know. I'm pretty good at picking up on these things and it's got me so nervous."

Nia just nodded.

"Hey, you know medicine, right, Nia?" Sam asked, her eyes wide. "You can help me if they start saying things I don't understand."

"Oh, I don't know..."

Nia wondered how she'd gone from comforting Sam to Sam suggesting she actually go with her to the doctor. "I'm sure they'll explain everything to you in a way that makes sense."

"Still, can you come? I don't want to go by myself." She rubbed her arms like she was cold and gave Nia what could only be described as puppy-dog eyes.

Nia sighed quietly and nodded. "Yes, I'll go with you."

"Oh, thank you!" she threw her arms around Nia and hugged her tight. "My appointment is at 3. Meet me downstairs at 2:30?"

"I'll be there."

Later, when Felicia got back to the room, Nia told her that she wasn't going to make it to the study group that afternoon because she had to help Sam out.

"Since when are you and Sam best friends?" Felicia asked with her eyebrow raised.

"We're not, but you know how I am. I can't just let someone be in need and not help them. It's not how I'm built."

"I guess it's a good thing you're going to be a doctor then. That empathy comes in handy, huh?"

Nia checked the time on her phone. "I gotta get going. I was supposed to meet her downstairs a few minutes ago."

She quickly slipped on her shoes and went to the lobby to meet Sam.

***

"Samantha Luts?" the nurse with the clipboard called out.

"Right here." Sam stood and nodded for Nia to come with her.

"Is this your...?" The nurse peered at the two of them over the top of her glasses as if to say, *Family only beyond this point.*

Sam grabbed Nia's hand. "She's my friend. I want her here for this."

The nurse nodded and smiled. "Of course."

They went into a back room and Sam had a seat on the exam table, even though she was just getting results and no actual check-up. The nurse jotted down a few notes from Sam and told them the doctor would be in shortly to talk with her.

"How are you feeling?" Nia asked.

Sam was swinging her legs on the table and chewing on her bottom lip. "Nervous. I can't shake this feeling."

"Well, I'm here. So whatever happens, you at least have a friend in the room."

Sam nodded and took a deep breath. "Okay, you're right."

They sat in silence for a moment until they were both startled by a rapid *knock-knock* at the door. "Hi, Samantha," he said gently, reaching out to give her a warm handshake. He looked a bit startled to see Nia sitting there but he recovered quickly and reached out his hand. "Hi, I'm Dr. Daniels."

"This is my friend, Nia," Sam said quickly. "She came here with me today for support."

Dr. Daniels nodded and Nia thought she could see a look of relief come over his face, as if he was glad a friend would be there for her after delivering this bad news. *Maybe Sam was right to ask me to come.*

"Well, I don't want to waste too much time so let's cut right to the chase." He sat on a stool across from Sam and clasped his hands in front of his body.

"We got your results back from your testing we did two weeks ago and unfortunately, Samantha, your test for HIV came back positive."

Sam nearly slid off the table. "Wait, what?"

"I'm sorry, Samantha." He held her hands in his for a moment. "The good news is that treatment has really improved over the years, and your quality of life will be much better. It is not a death sentence anymore, but it will require us to work together as a team, to make sure you are on the right medications so you can live a fairly regular life. I know this is a lot to take in right now, and you may be feeling overwhelmed. I have some information I'll give you for a local support group in case you're interested."

Sam just sat there, stunned.

Dr. Daniels turned to look at Nia and nodded toward Sam. "Would you two like a minute alone?"

"Yes, let me talk to her," Sam said.

Dr. Daniels got up and closed the door behind him.

Nia opened her mouth to speak but nothing she was thinking of saying sounded like any comfort. HIV? This was the big time. This wasn't chlamydia, which several of her friends had gotten over the past few years. That actually had a cure. No, this was serious. And Nia wasn't sure how to comfort someone who had just been told everything in her life was about to change.

Instead of saying anything, Nia just rubbed Sam's back while Sam cried into her hands.

"How did this happen?" Sam said to no one in particular. "This can't be happening."

"I think that the important thing right now is to not beat yourself up," Nia said carefully. "You'll get through this."

Sam sniffled and wiped her eyes on the hem of her shirt. "This is probably going to be the worst day of my life," she said calmly. "This right here is it."

Nia hated how tongue-tied she was. *What type of doctor am I going to be if I can't think of anything to say after a patient gets bad news?* She tried again. "You'll get through this. I promise."

Suddenly Sam lifted her head up and hopped down off the table. "I have to get out of here."

"Don't you want to wait until the doctor comes back so he can tell you what's next?"

"Nia." Her voice was breaking and Nia could see how red her eyes were from all the tears. "Nia. What am I going to do?"

"I'll tell you what you're going to do." She stood directly in front of Sam and grabbed her by the shoulders, easing her back down onto the table. "You're going to take some deep breaths, you're going to close your eyes, and you're going to hold my hand. We're going to sit here together and wait for Dr. Daniels to come back in. Then he's going to tell you what's next and you're going to do that. Okay?"

Sam sniffled again. "Okay."

They sat there quietly for about twenty minutes until a much more gentle knock came and Dr. Daniels poked his head in. "Is this a good time?" he asked.

Nia nodded and waved him in. As he sat down and talked to Sam about her options, Nia took in how he interacted with her. He was kind and patient, and he answered all her questions without making her feel rushed. *That's the kind of doctor I want to be,* Nia thought.

By the time they left the doctor's office, Sam's crying had slowed to a quiet sniffle.

She had stopped talking altogether and Nia thought it was best if she drove the both of them home. When they got to the parking lot, Nia turned the car off and went to open the door.

"No, wait." Sam reached out her hand. "Can you just...sit with me for a while? I can't go inside yet."

Nia leaned back in her seat. "Sure. I'll sit with you."

***

Nia and Mya continued their Thursday afternoon hangouts whenever they both had the day free. That Thursday, Mya wanted Nia to come over to Camille's apartment. She'd had Davis Jr. at the beginning of Nia's sophomore year and now the little guy was just over two years old. She had moved to the Castleberry Hill Apartments with her boyfriend Davis while she was pregnant. Shortly after DJ was born, they split up, but until recently they'd still lived together for the sake of co-parenting. Now that Davis had moved out, Camille was getting a feel for what single motherhood was all about and from what Mya had told her, she wasn't enjoying it very much.

"Come with me," Mya urged. "I'm heading over to Camille's to see how she's doing. You haven't seen DJ in a couple months — he got so big!"

Camille looked exhausted and frazzled when she opened the door. "Come in, come in," she said, kicking toys off to the side and creating a path for them to enter. The TV was loud and on Nickelodeon, with DJ sitting cross-legged in the middle of the room, bouncing along to the song in the show.

"DJ, you want to say hi to your Aunt Mya and Auntie Nia?"

At hearing his name, DJ pushed himself up on his little chubby toddler legs and ran over to wrap himself around Mya. "Heh-wo," he said, squeezing her knees.

"What's up, little buddy?" Mya picked him up and put him on her hip, looking at ease with her play nephew. He grabbed her face and kissed her a few times in a row.

"That's his new thing now," Camille said, scooping up toys and dumping them into a laundry basket. "He's just kissing any and everybody, so you gotta keep an eye on him."

"That's okay—you can give your auntie all the kisses you want," Mya cooed at DJ. He grinned and turned to Nia, reaching out his arms to climb into her embrace.

"Whoa, he's heavier than I thought," Nia said, struggling to get him settled in her arms.

"That's 'cause all he does is eat," Camille said, collapsing on the couch. "It's all I can do to keep that boy full!"

"So how is it going?" Nia said, sitting down on the floor with DJ, jiggling him in her lap.

"Eh, it's going," Camille replied. "I'm so tired, y'all. I feel like I barely get to sit still. I'm running from class to work to home and back again every day. I feel like I'm on a hamster wheel."

Mya sat next to Camille and rubbed her back. "That sounds draining, girl."

"It is. And I'm the only one who has a kid, so I just feel like I have no one to talk to about things I'm going through or how hard it is being a single mom."

"Didn't what's-her-name have a baby?" Nia closed her eyes and snapped her fingers. "Carmen, I think her name was?"

Mya shook her head. "Yeah but she went back home to Detroit."

"I love y'all but you don't have kids," Camille continued, "which means your day is whatever you want it to be. You don't have to completely change all of your plans because your kid got sick or your child's father suddenly is too busy to watch his own child. I know your lives are busy too, but mine is...complicated."

"What's going on with you and Davis? What do you mean he's too busy to watch DJ?"

"Ever since we broke up he's been acting funny. One week he's father of the year and the next it's like DJ doesn't exist. I never know who I'm dealing with, and it's so frustrating."

"We may not be able to relate, but we're here for you," Mya insisted.

"And I appreciate that," Camille said. "I really do. It's just that I can never get a babysitter to do anything other than work or go to class. I'd love someone to come over and watch DJ so just I can sleep or I don't know, go get my hair done."

Before Nia or Mya could say anything Camille began to cry softly.

"Hey, girl, it's okay!" Mya wrapped Camille in a big hug.

"I know it will be," Camille said, wiping her eyes. "I just had to let that out. It's a lot to keep to myself, you know?"

DJ climbed in his mom's lap and stuck his index finger in his mouth. "Mama, I'm hun-gee," he mumbled, nestled under her chin.

"Okay, baby, Mommy will get you a snack." She moved to get him a snack but Mya put out her hand to stop her.

"You know what?" Mya peeled DJ off his mom's lap and nodded her head toward the door. "We got this. Go. We'll watch DJ for a couple hours. You need a break."

"Oh, I don't know," Camille said. She looked down at her sweatpants and faded T-shirt. "I don't even know what I'd do with my free time."

"You're about to find out," Mya said. "Up you go." She shifted DJ to one hip and used her free arm to lift Camille off the couch.

"Okay, let me go change."

Five minutes later Camille was back, with her hair brushed back into a ponytail and the sweatpants exchanged for jeans and a sweater. "I'm going to go get a pedicure," Camille said, looking down at her toes. "I am so overdue."

"Enjoy yourself," Mya said, using DJ's arm to have him wave goodbye to his mom. "Can you say bye-bye?"

"Bye, bye, mama!" DJ shrieked, his adorable little toddler face wet with drool.

"Bye baby!" Camille said, blowing him a kiss. She grabbed her purse and phone off the table. "I'll be back in about an hour."

"Take your time," Mya called after her.

After Camille left, Mya got up and handed DJ to Nia. "Let me go see what this little boy can eat for a snack."

A few minutes later she came back with some crackers and juice in a sippy cup. They sat quietly and played, turning to DJ's favorite shows and using the crackers to teach him his numbers. "Say 'one,'" Mya prompted, laying out one cracker. She added another. "Say 'two'." DJ clapped every time he got one right.

Soon they heard the keys jingling in the lock and in walked Camille, her eyes bright.

Aside from her now hot pink toes, she looked like a whole new woman. "Thank y'all so much for watching him. I rarely get a chance to just be without worrying about where DJ is or how he's doing, so I appreciate you watching him for me."

"That's what we do, right?" Mya smiled at Nia. "We help each other out."

Let's Talk

If you've taken anything from this book so far, I hope you recognize that your future is what you make it. All of these characters—Nia, April, Patrice, Mya, Camille, Sam—make different decisions that lead them to different paths. Some of those paths, like Camille's, lead to early motherhood, where the challenges of becoming a woman and beginning your career can be made more difficult by the fact that you are also responsible for the well-being of another person. Other paths, like Nia's, lead to long nights and sacrifices to get where you want to go. It may not be easy for Nia to pass up on dating cute boys or studying until she falls asleep, but she has a goal and she's willing to do almost anything to get there.

I want to take a moment to talk about Samantha, the young woman who contracted HIV. Of course, it only takes one bad decision to wind up with HIV or any other STD; however, as a doctor I'd be remiss if I didn't tell you that sleeping around with multiple people increases your risk of catching a disease. It can feel good in the moment, but that moment can cost you. Ask yourself, "Is this worth it?"

Now, while HIV is a life-changing diagnosis, it doesn't necessarily have to be life-ending, as the doctor explained to Samantha. HIV is still a significant challenge and your life will be split into two segments—before your diagnosis and after. After the diagnosis, you have the huge challenge of managing your health with daily antiviral medication, informing your past sexual partners that they might have been exposed, figuring out how to inform your future sexual partners, and dealing with rejection as people fear the diagnosis. In addition, it's a financial burden when you take into account that the medication costs are huge, and it's much harder for you to get life insurance to protect yourself and loved ones. It's just not worth the risk.

I talk to a lot of young girls about college, but I want to remind you that college isn't the end goal. College is the time in your life where you discover who you are, what your talents are and how you can use that information to make a living for yourself. Don't take it too lightly — this is the foundation for the next 50 years of your life.

College is the time to prepare yourself for the real world. So choose everything carefully—your friends, the activities you get involved in, the people you date. All of that will have an impact years down the line.

What You Should Know – What Am I Good At?

When I speak in the community to young women, I'm always curious to see what they want to do with their lives. Do you know what you want to do?

Use this space to write your answers to these prompts:

I am happiest when I am:

I've always wondered what it would be like to:

I want to be known for:

My parents have told me I am good at:

My teachers have told me I am good at:

Chapter Ten: 2 Hearts

Nia felt the cool September breeze as she slung her bag over one shoulder with an arm full of notebooks and pens in the other, trudging her way across campus to the library as she'd already done many times during her first few weeks in medical school.

Once she got to the first floor she discovered that all the study pods—those coveted, practically soundproof rooms—were taken. She knew that students were only allowed to use them for four hours at a time, so she checked in with the library attendant. "When is the next available pod going to be open?" she asked impatiently.

The attendant chomped her gum and flipped through the sign-up pages. "Looks like room number three will be available at 2 p.m. You want me to pencil you in?"

She checked her phone. It was 1:15 now. She guessed she could wait. "Yes, please. Thanks."

She walked past the study pods slowly, hopefully trying to catch a student who was calling it a day a little bit earlier than their scheduled time. It was highly unlikely, since they were all first-year medical students trying to cram in as much studying time as possible, but Nia figured she would try anyway.

She turned and headed for the general study tables when she noticed a cute brown-skinned guy in the last study pod smile and give her a nod. He waved her over as if he knew her. She hesitated for a moment, then went over and opened the door.

"I'm Cory Patterson," he said, extending his hand to shake Nia's. Nia shifted her books to her other arm and shook his hand. "How are you doing?"

"I'm tired," Nia said, surprising herself with how honest she was being.

He laughed. "I feel you. I'm barely keeping my eyes open. You're in gross anatomy with me, right?"

She squinted, trying to place him. "Yeah, I saw you Tuesday, right? Your group was clowning you."

He nodded. "Yup. I was the guy doubling up on gloves. My mom told me she used to wear two pairs to make sure her hands didn't smell like formaldehyde."

"Your mom's a doctor?"

"Yup. Internal medicine over at the Cleveland Clinic."

"Oh, wow. So that means you're pretty familiar with all this. Being a doctor, I mean."

"Kind of. My mom had me pretty early in her career, so I remember going up to her office a lot as a kid. Her patients loved me. My dad, he works at Oberlin College in their history department."

"A doctor and a professor, huh? That's pretty impressive."

He shrugged. "They did alright. Worked really hard. They were the first in their families to go to college."

"I'm impressed."

"So what about you?" Cory said. "What do your people do?"

The books in Nia's hands were getting heavy, so she rested them on the table. Cory noticed her discomfort right away.

"Oh, man, I'm sorry. I should have invited you to sit down first. My bad. I saw you were looking for a space to study. I'm pretty quiet, so you are more than welcome to sit in here with me," he said, offering a big smile.

"You sure?"

He gestured to the table. "Sure. More than enough space for two. Don't want you to have to wait when there's half the table available."

Nia slid into the empty seat across from Cory and nodded her thanks. "Well, my mom is a nurse. My dad works at Boral Brick."

"Nice, nice. They sound like hard-working people, got a daughter in medical school. You're from Spelman, right?"

"How'd you know that?" Nia raised an eyebrow.

Cory held out his hands as if to say, *Whoa, trust me.* "I asked around. Saw you earlier, thought you were cute."

Nia blushed. "Thank you."

"I asked because I went to Hampton," he continued. "Been having a hard time adjusting to this campus. Hard going from a HBCU to a school with only a handful of us. You adjusting okay?"

"I think so." She pulled out one of her highlighters and notebooks. "I haven't really had time to think about it. They've got us so busy memorizing everything there is to know about medicine."

Cory nodded. "I know. There's so much to learn that I go to sleep thinking about Hesselbach's triangle from gross anatomy class."

That made Nia giggle. "I know. When I close my eyes all I see are arteries, veins, muscles, bones, and organs, organs, and more organs!"

They smiled at each other and Nia felt this calm, relaxed feeling fall over her. She had only recalled seeing Cory a few times before on campus, but she felt like she had known him for years. He had an easy-going nature to him and she could hardly remember the last time she had felt so at ease talking with a guy. He was refreshing.

But, cuteness aside, Nia had exams to get ready for. "Well, I'd better get started studying," she said, pulling out her laptop.

"Right, right. I promised I'd be quiet so…" He shut his mouth, smiled and turned back to his pile of papers.

Side by side they worked for a couple hours, Nia pausing every twenty minutes or so to stand up, stretch her arms to the sky and pace in circles. Cory just looked at her out the corner of his eye and smiled to himself.

"What?" Nia finally asked when she caught him grinning at her for the third time during one of her stand-and-stretch sessions.

"Nothing, it's just that I've never met anyone so disciplined," he said. He checked the time on his phone. "Every twenty minutes, like clockwork, you stand up and stretch. It's funny."

"Oh. It's just a habit I picked up," she explained, twirling her curls around her fingers nervously. "This counts as my exercise for the day." He laughed and went back to studying.

An hour later, Nia's eyes were starting to cross. She stood up and stretched, but this time she didn't sit back down.

"Hey, how much longer are you going to be here?" she asked, stifling a yawn.

"I dunno. Probably another hour or so." He gestured to his papers on the table.

"I'm going to run back to my apartment for like a half-hour. Can you watch my stuff? I just need to take a break. My eyes are tired."

"Of course."

Nia grabbed her purse and dug out her keys. "Thank you, I appreciate it."

By the time she got back to her small off-campus apartment, she wasn't sure if she'd make it back to the library. She collapsed face-first on the couch and just lay there for ten minutes, feeling like if she closed her eyes she might sleep for twenty four hours straight.

She slipped a bottle of water and an apple into her purse and took a deep calming breath before heading back to the library.

When she got back to the study pod, Cory had his eyes closed, looking like he was either sleeping or on his way there. "Cory?"

He jumped. "Oh, wow. I didn't even realize I had fallen asleep."

She smiled. "That's why I took a break because I would have been knocked out too. If you want, you can take a break and I'll watch your stuff for you."

He shook his head and started gathering up his belongings. "Nah, that's my signal for me to call it a day. When my body starts doing its own thing and shutting down without permission, that means I've had enough." He touched two fingers to his temple to give Nia a salute. "You keep doing your thing. I'll see you around."

As he brushed by Nia to leave, she got a whiff of his cologne and swooned a bit inside. He didn't smell like a lot of these guys around here, with their cheap body sprays. He smelled like a *man* and Nia was definitely interested in a guy who could match her maturity.

She smiled a little on the inside and got back to studying. When she got back to her apartment later on, she was trying hard not to think about Cory, but failing. *I wonder if he lives nearby*, she thought to herself. *Maybe I'll ask him on Tuesday.*

Nia heated up some leftover pizza for dinner and chewed it absentmindedly while she flipped through the mail. *Bills, bills, junk.*

Just once she'd like to have some mail that wasn't just companies asking for money.

She hadn't intended to come to Case Western Reserve University for medical school, but after researching, she decided it was time to get away from Atlanta for a bit and spread her wings. Cleveland seemed like the quiet sort of city that would be perfect for Nia's personality. Her mom and dad were happy to see her move on to the next chapter, but she could tell that they missed her already. There were no more weekly or even monthly visits like when she was at Spelman, so they relied on FaceTime or Skype to stay in touch. PJ was growing like a weed, now a high school freshman on the basketball team. She hated that she was missing his games now, but she texted him before every game to tell him how proud she was of him.

Nia dug into her bag to grab her phone and felt her fingertips brush against a random slip of paper. *That wasn't in there before, was it?* Nia wondered. She pulled it out and unfolded it.

It was a note from Cory. *Not sure if you're dating much these days or if you already have someone special in your life, but I'd love to take you out to dinner sometime. I didn't get a chance to ask for your number, so here's mine. If you're not interested, that's cool too and we can just be friends. Either way, I'll see you on Tuesday.*

"Wow," Nia said out loud. She stared at the paper for a minute, which faintly smelled like Cory's cologne and then set it down on the table. She grabbed her phone and texted Patrice: *Girl, I met this fine brotha today and he asked me out on a date! Like, a real smooth "let me take you out to dinner" date. Not just Netflix and chill.*

Patrice texted back almost instantly: *Girl, does he have a brother? A cousin? A young-but-equally-cute uncle? Hook me up!*

Nia giggled: *I'll see what I can do.*

Nia went to the bathroom to start her bedtime routine, which she hoped would give her enough time to figure out what to say to Cory. Every night, to help her relieve the stress of medical school she took a steaming hot shower while playing music with a few candles lit to set the mood.

Then she used her favorite cocoa butter cream to moisturize her skin from head to toe, making sure to give her body a nice massage before she slipped on her pajamas, wrapped up her hair and got into bed.

She pulled her phone from her side table and debated whether she should call or text Cory. She figured a text would be fine: *Hey, I got your note. I'd love to have you take me to dinner.*

She quickly slipped her phone back on the table and eased down into the comforter. She hadn't been this excited for a date in a while, and already she was thinking about what she would wear. Just then her phone buzzed, interrupting her thoughts. *Great. I was thinking I could take you out tomorrow. Is 6 p.m. okay?*

She grinned so hard she could feel her dimples showing. *6 sounds perfect. I'll see you then.*

***

"You sure you're going to be okay in those?" Nia asked, laughing. They had walked to dinner at Valerio's, this little Italian restaurant just a few blocks from campus. On the way back to Nia's apartment, they stopped at Corner Alley, the bowling alley and bar around the corner. Cory had bet that he could beat her in ten frames and Nia, never one to back down from a challenge, accepted. But when they got to the counter, they didn't have size 11 shoes for Cory so he was trying to squeeze into size 10.

"If I lose I'm blaming the shoes," he said, winking at Nia. He picked up an orange ball and handed it to her. "This one looks about your size."

"Thanks." They set up and started taking turns, Cory easily coming out ahead after a few frames.

"Doesn't look like the shoes are stopping you," she said, sipping her Sprite.

"I gotta tell ya, my toes are killing me," he admitted. They shared a laugh and he rolled again. "Ah, right in the gutter."

"It's okay, I've been letting you win so far. Now it's time I stop kidding around."

"Is that right?"

"I'm serious! I could be a pro-bowler but I figured more money was in medicine, so here I am." Nia picked up her ball, steadied herself in the middle of the lane and threw a perfect strike. She turned around slowly and posed. "I told you. I'm good."

"Okay, okay. I see you how you play." Cory got up and knocked down seven pins, just enough to keep him in the lead.

"So I'm going to call this one a strike too. Not even going to watch them all fall." Nia threw the ball down the lane and turned before the ball reached the pins to look at Cory's face as he watched her second strike in a row.

"Are you messing with me right now?" he said, laughing. "You some kind of bowling prodigy?"

She shrugged. "Nah. My dad used to take me bowling all the time. It was really serious daddy-daughter bowling time. He showed me proper form, strategy, all that."

"So you're a daddy's girl, huh?"

Usually when people asked Nia that question she would feel defensive. But she could tell Cory wasn't judging her; he simply wanted to get to know her better.

"You could say that," she responded.

"That's cool. I'm pretty tight with both my parents so I get how it is. Especially now, right? You kind of need your parents in a way you didn't before." He threw what looked like a perfect strike, but the ball veered at the last minute and only knocked down three.

Nia smiled to herself and picked up the ball, again rolling a perfect strike.

By the time the game ended, Nia had beaten him handily, but Cory was good-natured about it, teasing her about how she could go pro.

They walked across the street and passed Mitchell's, a local ice cream shop with all types of amazing flavors. Nia had quickly fallen in love with its key lime pie flavor her first week on campus and tried to get at least one scoop every week. So when Cory nodded his head toward the entrance and asked if she'd like to get some, she practically beat him to the cashier.

"Double scoop in a waffle cone, please," she said, digging in her purse to get her card to pay.

"No, I got this," he said, gesturing for her to put away her wallet.

He grabbed his and looked at the menu board. "What's the best flavor?" he asked Nia.

"I love all of them, but my favorite is the key lime pie."

"I'll try that then. One scoop please. Waffle cone."

They got their ice cream and sat down on one of the benches outside, relieved that summer hadn't turned too quickly into fall, the temperature hovering in the low 70s.

"This is pretty good," he said, raising the cone as if to offer a toast. "I'm not that much of an ice cream guy, but this hits the spot."

"You know, actually, I'm not either, but this place reminds me of my favorite ice cream shop down in Atlanta. I come here when I'm feeling homesick."

"So how often are you here?"

"About once a week." They burst out laughing.

"You really miss your folks, huh?"

Nia thought for a minute. "It's not that I miss them. I miss everything about Atlanta. But that's only natural, right? I spent the first twenty-two years of my life there. I'm still trying to learn this city, trying to remember to say 'pop' instead of 'coke.'"

Cory laughed. "You Southern girls are so cute."

"Where are you from?" she asked, switching topics. "I know your parents live here but where are you from originally?"

"Detroit," he said, taking a bite out of the waffle cone. "Moved here in high school. My mom got a job at the Cleveland Clinic, so we all moved here."

Nia was shocked. "So, your dad moved so your mom could take her dream job?"

"Yup. You sound surprised."

"I am. I don't hear a lot about men following their wives. I always hear about women following their husbands, or boyfriends, even. But that's good that he was willing to do that."

"Hey, a woman with her own career can't be anything but good, right? The way I see it, it just makes you a power couple. I'm not threatened by a strong woman."

Nia tried hard not to melt right off the bench. "Good to know."

They finished their cones and went to toss their napkins in the trash. They turned in the direction of Nia's apartment and began the slow, five-minute walk. "So I've been thinking ever since we were at dinner that I wanted to ask you out again," Cory admitted. "I hope you don't think that makes me sound thirsty."

"Not at all. I think it's cute."

He nodded.

"Well, I know that it's our first year of med school so we're both going to be crazy busy, but I just wanted to put that out there."

"Well, you have my number. Call me. We'll get together."

They reached the front steps to her apartment and stood there smiling at each other.

"What?" she said, blushing.

"Nothing." Cory just kept looking at her and smiling harder.

"See, we can't just be staring at each other like some fools," Nia said, laughing. "You want to come up? We could kick it in the lounge area."

"Nah, I'll let you go. I've got a bunch of stuff I have to do before class tomorrow. But I will call you. We'll get that second date set up."

Nia smiled and grabbed her keys out of her purse. As she was looking down, Cory swooped up and gave her a quick peck on the cheek. "Thanks for coming out with me tonight," he said.

"I had a great time. Glad you got to try my favorite ice cream."

"It was good. I have a new favorite now." They hugged goodbye and he waited on the sidewalk until she was safely inside. She waved from the door and he started down the street to his apartment complex, a couple blocks away.

She just got into her apartment and slipped off her shoes when her phone buzzed. It was a text from Cory: *I think I really like you.*

She held the phone to her chest and beamed. Then she reminded herself to play it cool.

She waited a few minutes and typed out a quick response: *I think I really like you too.*

Let's Talk

Nia's working really hard toward her goal of becoming a doctor. I've been in her shoes and I have to tell you —it's a long, hard path. I went to school for over twenty years —eight of those solely focused on becoming a doctor. It included many long nights like Nia's experiencing. I never fell asleep on a date, but I came pretty close a few times.

I did what I had to do in order to reach my goal. It was important to me that I finished what I started and because I pressed forward, even through the difficult times, I can say proudly that I am a doctor today, and I've been practicing for fifteen years.

Do you have the type of persistence needed to reach your goals? Whether you want to be a doctor or an engineer or a teacher, there will be times along your path where you might feel like it would be easier to give up and do something else. Nothing worth having comes easy. Every person you admire, whether it's a celebrity or someone from your neighborhood, had to work hard to get to where they are.

So I ask young people like you all the time: how bad do you want it? Do you want to reach your goal bad enough that you are willing to make sacrifices? Maybe you can't hang out with your friends every weekend because you need to study or practice those days. Maybe you have to say no to a couple of dates with cute guys. Maybe you have to work longer hours than other people. It might feel unfair. You might wonder why you're working so hard at certain points.

Whatever you do, don't quit. If you quit, you're back to square one, and the hard work starts all over again.

The late heavyweight boxer Muhammad Ali said it best, "I hated every minute of training, but I said, 'Don't quit. Suffer now and live the rest of your life as a champion.'" If you keep pressing on, you will be the one who has the career you've always wanted, the fancy car, the house, the awards, the life you deserve.

So don't give up. Don't quit.

What You Should Know – The Success Blueprint

What does success look like for you? Do you know? If you don't know where you want to go, it's a lot harder to get there. Take a few moments to follow these writing prompts to get a little clarity on your definition of success:

I admire:

They are successful to me because they:

The one thing that I can learn from them is how to:

Three things I can do today to get closer to my goals are:

Chapter Eleven: Countdown 4,3,2,1...

"We are going to be late!" Cory called from the other room. Nia slipped on some small gold hoop earrings and came into the living room. "How do I look?"

Cory nodded his approval. "You look great, Nia."

Nia was nervous. It was Match Day, the day that medical students all over the country find out where they will be heading to work after medical school. As stressful as the previous four years had been, there was a bit of comfort in knowing a place and having bonded with their fellow students. Now they were about to move on to a new environment with new pressures, and Nia was just about ready to throw up from the excitement.

The added pressure was that Cory and Nia hoped to be matched together. Their relationship had progressed deeply over the course of medical school. Since that first date, the two of them had been inseparable, first as close friends, and then it evolved into a deep love. Nia knew it was love the first time she let Cory pick her up from her apartment for a date. She trusted him completely, and he had never done anything to cause her to question that trust in the four years she had known him.

He was a consistent source of support, having been there for her during sophomore year, when her father had a heart attack unexpectedly. Cory emptied his savings to buy her a plane ticket to get there that afternoon and came to be with her the next day. Thankfully, her father was better now, and Nia had never forgotten how quickly Cory had come to her aid when they were still relatively new boyfriend and girlfriend.

It was surprising to her that they managed to make it three years without having sex. Nia was as shocked as anyone to find herself a 25-year-old virgin. But on one of their early dates, Cory told her that he was celibate after witnessing some rough relationships in his circle. She almost fell off her chair to hear a guy as cute as Cory tell her that he was waiting until he found "the one" to have sex. When she told him she was celibate too, she was delighted to see the smile that spread across his face.

They had an undeniable chemistry though. She felt her pulse quicken every time he stepped into the room and he admitted he had a hard time taking his eyes off her curves. So they had to set up some ground rules if they wanted to remain celibate. The first was that they had to take their dates out in public. They very rarely stayed in to just kick it on the couch, even though most of the time they were exhausted and would have preferred just taking a nap together. The second rule was that they would find other ways to be intimate together. Nia found that the sexiest thing she did with Cory was talk. They would have these amazing conversations about everything, and he was always making her laugh. After a date once, she found she could hardly stand up straight because her stomach hurt so much from all the laughing she did.

Still, they'd come close to slipping up a few times. Nia felt her resolve getting weaker by the day, but luckily today there would be no such temptation. They were on their way to the student center, where the Match Day ceremony would be taking place. Every year, all the medical students gathered with their friends and loved ones and waited until noon to grab the envelope that let them know where they would be spending the next few years of their lives doing their internships and residency training in their chosen medical specialty. Both Nia and Cory hoped to get matched at University Hospitals, right there in Cleveland, but there was no guarantee.

"I feel like I'm about to faint," Nia admitted.

"Me too," he said. "But no matter what happens, we'll both be good, right?"

"Right." She grabbed his hand and led him out of her apartment and into the cool air.

Cleveland winters had taken a while to get used to, but this one had been kind of mild. Nia chuckled to herself that she had been in the

Midwest long enough that she knew a temperature in the 40s as mild. Even though it was March, it did not yet feel like spring. Her Southern parents would have just shaken their heads at her.

She wished they could have come today, but she understood that they'd have to save their money for plane tickets to graduation in a few months. She promised to call them after she matched to tell them where she'd be headed.

Once they arrived at the student center, the room was buzzing with their fellow students anxiously staring at the clock. Nia spotted Felicia in the crowd and waved as she made her way over.

"I'm so excited I'm about to throw up," Felicia said as a greeting.

"Me too," Nia said.

Cory let out a long breath. "We're going to be fine," he said, more to himself than anyone else.

Felicia and Nia linked arms as the dean called the ceremony to order. "Welcome students, family, faculty, and staff. This is a special day for all of you. I personally just want to congratulate you on making it to this milestone in your career. Every single one of your professors and I are so proud of the hard work you've put in to get to this moment. We expect to shed a lot of tears of joy as we discover where this class of amazing students is headed next."

The atmosphere was bubbling and Nia took slow, deep breaths as she waited. "As is tradition," the dean continued, "students will open their envelopes at exactly noon, the same time as all other students across the country. Get your cameras ready as these are once-in-a-lifetime moments ahead of you."

Everyone glanced toward the clock on the wall at the same time. 11:58.

"Come on!" someone from the crowd shouted and everyone laughed.

"Time for the countdown," the dean said and he started them off. "10…9… 8…7…6…5…4…3…2…1!"

The staff took down the barrier surrounding the table with the envelopes and each of the medical students went up to grab theirs. Cory grabbed his and Nia's and brought them over to where she was sitting.

"Same time?" he asked.

She nodded and they ripped them open together.

"University Hospitals!" she shouted and he flipped his papers around to show her his. "Same!"

They hugged and kissed and she felt like everything was falling into place. Her friends came over to her and shared their news. Some were headed to Chicago, Boston, or Baltimore and they were all happy and overcome with joy.

She looked for Felicia, who was jumping for joy in the corner. "I got Emory, girl!"

"What? Congratulations!" Nia knew that was Felicia's first choice.

"I gotta call my mom," she said, which reminded Nia that she hadn't yet called her parents. They knew the ceremony was at noon so they promised to be waiting by the phone.

"Mom, dad?" she said once they picked up.

"We're here!" her mom said impatiently. "Where are you headed?"

"University Hospitals!" she yelled into the phone.

"Congratulations honey! That's where you wanted to go, right? Where is Cory headed? Did you get matched at the same place?"

"We did!"

"That is fantastic news," her dad said. "I'm so proud of you. I wish we could be there."

"What is all the noise in the background?" Nia asked. "Are you guys at home?"

"No, we're in the car," her mom said quickly.

"Together?"

"Yes, together. You are so nosy," her dad said, laughing.

"Well, I just wanted to call you like I said I would and let you know. I should be able to come home in a few weeks so I'll see you then?"

"Okay, sweetheart. We'll see you then. And congratulations again! We're proud of you!"

Nia hung up and found Cory on the phone with his parents. He seemed to be whispering something so she couldn't hear. As she came closer, he abruptly hung up and looked like he had just gotten caught doing something.

"Was that your parents?" she asked.

"Yup. They're really happy," he said. "They wanted me to tell you congratulations."

He looked a little shifty, but Nia let it slide. "Aw, that's nice. Are they coming down?"

"No, my mom had work and my dad has a class now. But I'll see them later."

The crowd had started to thin a bit, and the noise level dropped considerably.

"You need to go rest up," Cory said, hugging Nia tightly and nuzzling her neck. "I've got a bunch of plans for us tonight to celebrate. And I don't want to hear any excuses about how you're tired." "Oh, please," Nia said, stepping back so she could get a good look at him. "If anything, you're the one who's always tired."

"Nah, I'm serious," Cory said. He took her hands in his and kissed them gently. "Go home; take a nap, a shower, whatever you have to do to feel rested."

"Alright." Nia did feel a little tired, so she kissed him goodbye and headed back to her apartment. She nestled herself into her big thick comforter and almost smiled herself to sleep. Everything was going great and she was excited to be on her way to achieving her goal of being a doctor and she had a fine, smart man who loved her too!

A couple hours later Nia woke up to a text message from Cory: *Meet me at Valerio's at 7, bae.* It was just about 5 p.m. so Nia rested her eyes again. She was still floating from everything that had happened that day. *Is this my life?* She asked herself.

She pulled herself to a sitting position and grabbed her phone to text Felicia: *Girl, can you believe this? I mean, can you believe it?*

A few seconds later her phone buzzed: *Not at all, girl. I'm so happy I've been crying all day. LOL.*

Nia slipped on her favorite blue blazer and skinny jeans as she headed out to the restaurant. She was ready to celebrate her big day with Cory and wondered what surprises he had up his sleeve. "Right this way," the hostess said, gesturing for Nia to follow. But instead of leading her to the general dining area, the hostess kept going toward the back of the restaurant, through the double doors that led to the upstairs area.

As Nia followed behind her, she began to feel a bit anxious. *Where are we going*, she wondered.

At the top of the stairs, the hostess moved to the side so Nia could see the full view of the room. There stood her mother, her father and PJ, each with a dozen gorgeous red roses in their hands. Behind them was a host of her friends from college and a few of Cory's relatives. His mom and dad stood off to the side, smiling wide.

"Mom, Dad, what are you doing here?" Nia exclaimed, rushing across the room to hug them.

She turned to PJ and gave her little brother (who'd had a major growth spurt since the last time she saw him) a big embrace. "What are you doing here, dude?"

"It's your special day," her mom said, smiling wide. "We wanted to be here to celebrate."

"Aw, I thought you wouldn't be able to make it for Match Day," Nia said, tears beginning to well up in her eyes.

"Well, it's your special day," her dad said, echoing her mom. "We couldn't miss this. When you called us earlier we were on our way from the airport."

"These are for you," PJ said, handing Nia the roses.

"Wow, I can't believe this." She looked to see all the people in the room. "But where is Cory?"

As soon as she said that, the lights dimmed a bit and a soft R&B instrumental started playing. Cory came out from the stairwell, behind Nia. He looked every bit as handsome as the first day they met.

Nia felt a presence behind her and she turned to see Cory, standing there with the biggest smile on his face. "Oh, my God," she whispered.

"Hey, beautiful," he said, taking the roses from her arms and placing them on the table next to her. "I gathered all your friends and family and some of my friends and family to be here to witness this. I've loved you since that day in the library, when I met you as this ambitious, first-year med student. You were funny and confident and the most beautiful woman I had ever seen. I knew then that if you gave me a chance, I wouldn't mess it up."

He held her hands softly and continued. "And since that first date, I've been sprung for you, girl. You have helped me make it through medical school, while handling your own business as a med student and I cannot thank you enough for that. You make me a better man every day because of who you are and how you love me."

Nia clasped her hands over her mouth as Cory dropped to one knee. He dug in his pocket and pulled out a red velvet box and popped it open. Inside was a beautiful gold band with a small cluster of diamonds in the center. Nia thought it was the most beautiful ring she had ever seen. "Nia, would you do me the honor of being my wife?"

"Yes! Yes, I will."

Cory rose to his feet and swept Nia up in a big embrace, lifting her off the ground. He kissed her gently on the lips and squeezed her even tighter. He took her left hand in his and slipped the ring on her finger. "This was my grandmother's ring," he said, whispering in Nia's ear. "My mother thought you should have it."

Nia held her hand out and admired the beautiful diamonds. "I can't believe this is all happening. I really thought today couldn't get any better, but you have surprised me, Cory."

"I always do," he said with a wink. Nia's father came up to him and gave him a strong embrace and pat on the back. PJ followed close behind, doing his best to emulate his dad's protective nature.

Nia's mom rushed up to her daughter and gave her a big hug and a kiss on both cheeks. "You are going to be the most beautiful bride," she said. "Oh, I can't wait to see you walk down that aisle. And what a handsome man you'll be walking toward!"

"Oh God, mom." Nia blushed.

"I'm going to have some beautiful grandbabies!" her mom joked. "And smart too!"

"Let's go get you something to drink," PJ said, coming up behind his mom and slinging an arm over her shoulder. He winked at his sister and steered her over to the bar.

Cory's parents came over from their spot on the sidelines.

His mom squeezed Nia's hands and beamed.

"I'm so happy my son is marrying a smart girl like you," she said. "Three doctors in the family. I'm so blessed."

His dad smiled and slipped an arm around his wife's waist. "Yes, Nia welcome to the family. We're so thrilled for you two."

Well-wishers came up to Nia and Cory all night, showering the lovebirds with advice and tips on wedding planning and marriage.

Cory's parents had sprung for an elaborate feast, so all the guests dined on fresh pasta, delicious chicken and all types of Italian desserts.

Toward the end of the night, after most of the guests had left, Nia leaned against Cory's chest and sighed happily. "This was perfect," she told him.

"I'm glad you enjoyed yourself. You're happy you took that nap earlier, aren't you?"

"I am!" she laughed. "You always seem to know me so well."

Cory just smiled and kissed her on the forehead.

***

"I cannot believe you got a ring without giving it up!" Patrice said, laughing and admiring Nia's engagement ring. A week after Match Day, Patrice flew into town for a belated celebration, upset she had missed the big engagement party itself. They went out for dessert and drinks at the Cheesecake Factory as Nia filled in all the details.

"I actually can't believe we've been together this long and we haven't had sex," Nia said.

"Some of your doctor colleagues need to study you two," Patrice joked. "But in all seriousness, how have you been with this guy for three years, as fine as he is, and you haven't wanted to jump his bones with the quickness?"

"Oh, I've definitely wanted to," Nia corrected her. "But we've been very clear about what we wanted — a strong, healthy relationship. You know sex complicates everything. I wanted him to actually see me. To want to get to know me without getting to see me naked."

"But three years, though?" Patrice scrunched up her face. "Whew! That is a long time."

Nia nodded. "I can't lie. I'm glad he put a ring on it because I cannot wait until our wedding night. I'm ready."

"I bet you are!" Patrice exclaimed. She pushed her key lime cheesecake around on her plate. "I'm mad I missed the engagement party."

"It was beautiful, girl. He had all our friends and family there. I just about floated out of the room I was so happy."

"Well, you definitely deserve it. Cory is an amazing guy. I just wish he had a brother."

They both laughed. "So what's the plan now?"

"The plan?"

"Yeah. You getting married this year or next year? You going to do a long engagement 'til you get done with your residency?"

Nia paused. "We haven't really talked about it yet. So I don't know."

"I say you just go and get married now. Do a little quick wedding. Intimate. For your family and close friends like me. You can do a big party or something later."

"Maybe. I've never been into the big fuss of a wedding."

"Girl, I was in my cousin's wedding last year and let me tell you —it was chaos. She had eleven bridesmaids! That means her husband had to find eleven groomsmen or the pictures would have looked all lopsided. So he found 11 random dudes and they were flaky as all get out. Half of them were grumbling the whole day, kept wandering off when it was time to take pictures.

I say skip all that nonsense and just make it about the two of you. That's what's most important, right?"

Nia nodded and took a bite of her Oreo cheesecake. "True."

"So what's happening with you? What's new?" Nia asked, polishing off the last bite of her dessert.

"I'm good. Working with this educational advocacy group now. They've got me working long hours, girl. But I like it. Feels like I'm using my brain for good. And it pays well, surprisingly. I might even be able to afford to get you a wedding gift."

"Ha!"

"But seriously girl, I'm proud of you. To think of how we used to talk all those years ago about what life would look like for us and now we're doing it! You're a doctor and got a fine doctor fiancé. I'm working with policymakers to fix this country's education system. This is what we've been working toward. Could you imagine this when we were in seventh, eighth grade?"

"Definitely not," Nia admitted. "Remember when we were obsessed with Bobby D?"

"Girl, I'm still obsessed with him," Patrice said, laughing. "Don't judge me!"

"This is great catching up with you," Nia said, turning serious. "I mean it. I miss you. So this was nice."

"I miss you too, girl. Hopefully the next time I see you will be before your wedding. I do get an invite, right?"

"Of course you get an invite. You're one of my oldest friends!"

"I'm just checking."

They paid for their cheesecake and parted ways. Nia left the restaurant thinking about the wedding. Should they just do a small ceremony? She knew her mother would be disappointed if she wasn't able to see her daughter get married in a big white princess dress with half of Atlanta in attendance, but that would be way too expensive. Nia hadn't really thought about what *she* wanted. She figured she would stop by Cory's place to discuss it.

"What's up, girl?" Cory said, as Nia let herself in. Since their engagement last week, he had given her a key to his place. She said she didn't want to live together until they got married, but he felt that she should at least have a key. She felt weird using it, but she had to admit that it felt like they were merging their lives together slowly, and she liked that feeling.

He was in the kitchen, loading the dishwasher and wiping down the counters. He was a neat freak; the only person Nia knew who insisted on washing the dishes as soon as they had finished cooking dinner. "Easier for me to relax if I know I don't have a sink full of dishes waiting for me," he had explained to her once. Dirty dishes had never gotten in the way of Nia's relaxation, though.

"So I've been thinking about this engagement?" she said, twirling the ring around her finger.

He stood straight up. "You're not changing your mind, are you?"

"No, nothing like that." She could see him physically relax. "I just left dinner with Patrice and she was asking about the wedding. She had some good questions."

"Like what?"

"Like, when are we getting married?"

Cory closed the dishwasher and turned it on. He wiped his hands on a dishtowel and took two steps across the small kitchen to stand directly in front of Nia. He wrapped his arms around her waist. "Let's get married today. Would you like that?"

"Be serious!" she said, laughing. "When should we get married?"

"I don't know." He took a step back and leaned against the counter. "What do you think?"

"Maybe right after graduation? Once we start residency it's going to be really tricky.

We won't really have time for a honeymoon or anything for a while."

Cory looked like he was considering it. "So in about three months? Done."

"Really?"

"Yeah. I told you, girl. I would marry you today.

So in three months I'll be there with a fly suit and a fresh line-up waiting for you at the altar." He rubbed his hands together.

"Let's do this. Pick the date."

"You're serious?" Nia hadn't expected the conversation to go this quickly from "When are we getting married" to "Pick a date."

"Girl…" Cory pulled out his phone and scrolled through his calendar. "Let's see…graduation is June 3. I'll marry you on June 11. How 'bout that?"

Nia smiled. "Okay."

"Look at that. Got a wedding date set. That's what a power couple does – we get ish done!" He turned to the counter to grab his dinner plate, piled high with spaghetti and meatballs. "You want some?"

"No, I told you, I just ate with Patrice."

"Oh, that's right. Well, you're welcome to sit and watch me eat," he said with a grin. He sat on the couch and patted the cushion next to him. Nia sat.

"So we don't have a lot of time," she began. "So we're thinking a small wedding? Here? In Atlanta? Detroit?"

"You want to get married in Atlanta?" he asked, a mouth full of food. He sounded surprised. Nia wiped a bit of the marinara sauce off his top lip.

"I do. Yeah."

He nodded and kept eating and talking. "Okay."

"You are being very laid back about all this," Nia remarked, raising an eyebrow.

Cory put down his plate and turned to face Nia. "Of course I am. The big decision has been made. I get to marry you. The rest is just details. We could get married in the middle of a field for all I care."

Nia melted. He had a habit of being very straightforward with his feelings, something Nia could never quite get used to. Previous guys she had dated never lasted too long because she didn't like playing guessing games. Cory had her heart from the beginning because he wasn't ever shy about letting her know exactly how he felt about her.

"Since we're getting married so quickly," Nia said, trying to sound nonchalant, "we should probably go get tested together. So we don't have to think about it later."

Cory raised an eyebrow. "Oh really?"

"Yeah."

"My last test was years and years ago," he said. "Came back all clear. But I'll take another one for you, no problem."

"Yes, because when you've seen what we've seen…" Nia said, shuddering at some of the patients she'd seen at the hospital.

He nodded. "I get it."

"Thank you. And I'll get tested too," she offered quickly. "So you're not just doing it alone."

He kissed her on the forehead. "Let's go tomorrow. I've got some time in the afternoon."

"Okay, sounds good."

Two weeks later Nia was in the passenger seat of Cory's car, trying to figure out where he was taking her for yet another surprise.

"These are horrible guesses," Cory said, laughing so hard Nia swatted him on the arm.

"Quit laughing at me!" she said with a smile.

"I'm going to start planning surprises and leaving you in the dark about everything."

"You can't keep a surprise," he said knowingly. Nia hushed because she knew it was true.

Soon they pulled up to their final destination, a rustic looking cabin in the midst of rural Ohio. "We're spending the night here?" Nia asked.

Cory nodded. "Yup. My friend told me about this place. He brought his girlfriend here a couple months ago to propose. It's really romantic inside. Don't freak out."

"No, I trust you," Nia said slowly, looking around. There was a hint of spring in the air and the snow around them had begun to thaw a bit in early April. "But I don't have any clothes."

"I packed some for you," he said, nodding toward the bag in the back. "I needed you to be really surprised."

"Well, I am," she said. "Good job again, Cory."

"What you'll love about this place is they deliver breakfast to you in the morning. A big ol' basket full of breakfast foods."

"Do they have waffles?" Nia would drop everything for a great waffle; it was one of her favorite foods.

"They do! I made sure before I made the reservation," he said.

"I really do love you," she said, standing on tip-toe to kiss him.

"That's because I feed you waffles," he said. He grabbed the bag out of the backseat and nodded toward the front door. "Ready to go in?"

Cory was right —the inside was much more modern looking than the exterior would suggest. There was a huge living room with solid oak floors, wine-colored furniture and a large flat-screen TV on one wall. The one bedroom, which was off the side of the modern kitchen, had a king-size bed and another flat-screen TV on the wall.

"So why did you bring me here?" Nia asked.

"Well, I wanted us to get away from school, from work, from everything and just be here to celebrate with each other," he said, taking her hand in his. "We've worked so hard these past few years, and I realized we've never been together overnight. We're working toward forever, right?"

"Yes," Nia said slowly.

"So I wanted some extended time with you." Cory said, "No rushing home at midnight. I got a couple movies, I brought some food for dinner…let's just make some memories before we get married."

Nia eased onto one of the barstools in the kitchen while Cory unloaded the car with the groceries he had picked up before he got to her apartment. "I hope you like shrimp pasta," he said. "'Cause that's what I got."

"Sounds delicious."

"Glad you approve," he said with a wink.

After dinner they cuddled on the couch to watch a movie but Nia, being Nia, was so tired and full from dinner that she fell asleep on Cory's chest.

"Nia," he whispered, nudging her awake at the end of the movie. "Nia, wake up."

"Did I fall asleep?" she asked.

"Yup. Wipe the drool off your mouth," he joked.

"Oh, man, I drooled on your shirt." She laughed.

"It's cool. I gotta get used to it, right? Let's just get you to bed. You must be exhausted."

Nia slipped into the extra-large T-shirt Cory had packed for her and slipped into bed with him. Cory wore some pajama pants and a white shirt.

Nia suddenly felt vulnerable, as she realized she had never been horizontal with him before.

"What are you thinking?" he whispered.

"I'm thinking I've never been in bed with you before."

"Is that why you're all the way over there?"

Nia looked and realized that they could have fit a whole other person in the bed between them. She scooted closer, and Cory put his arm around her waist. "Is that okay?"

"It's good," she said and she nestled even closer, so that her chest was on his. She felt his heartbeat and realized she was holding her breath. She let it out slowly.

"We don't have to do anything you don't want to do," Cory said, attempting to straighten his shirt. "You're in the lead here."

Nia felt every ounce of resolve she had fall to the side. She wanted him, and she wanted him bad. She kissed him hard as her answer and pulled her shirt over her head.

"Wait, are we really going to do this?" Cory said, pulling back for a minute.

"Yes," she said firmly, reaching to kiss him again.

"I don't have a condom."

"What?" Nia was frustrated and fell back on her pillow.

"Well, I didn't plan on this so I didn't think we would have sex tonight."

"Go get one."

"What?"

"Go get one." She looked at the clock. "That store up the street? They'll have one, right?"

"Yeah," Cory said slowly. "Probably."

"Okay. I'll wait here. You go get one."

Cory slipped out of bed and put on his shoes. "I'll be back."

Nia sat straight up and pulled the covers to her chest and smiled as he headed out the door. *Oh my God I cannot believe we're about to have sex.*

She began to have second thoughts. *Man, I waited all this time. What's a couple more months until our wedding day?* Then she reminded herself that she always intended on waiting until she found someone worthy of being with. Cory definitely fit that bill and they were already engaged, so why not?

By the time Cory got back, she was firm in her decision to have sex and was ready to get started. He slipped back into bed, his body a little cold from the run to the store and Nia ran her hands over his arms to warm him up.

"Did you get it?" she asked.

"I did."

"Good." She kissed him slowly and they wrapped their arms around each other. "I love you."

Cory kissed her and eased her onto her back. "I love you too."

***

The next morning Nia thought she'd be sore, but she was okay. She stretched and turned to see Cory right next to her, practically on her pillow. She got up and grabbed her shirt from the floor and slipped on some pants. She was just in time, as she heard a quick knock at the door.

"Breakfast is here!" she said happily as she went to answer it.

Sure enough, one of the staff members held a huge basket in her hands, and she set it on the kitchen table. "Enjoy."

Nia opened the basket. The smell of waffles, bacon and fruit salad hit her nose. She went over to Cory and nudged him awake. "Hey, sleepyhead," she teased. "Breakfast is ready."

"They brought it already?" he asked sleepily. "Is it really in a basket?"

"Yup."

Nia hopped on a barstool and nibbled on a piece of the waffle, dipping it into a bit of syrup. "Man, these are so good. Try some."

They sat and ate for a minute, neither one talking about what happened the night before. They didn't need to. The night was perfect. Cory was so gentle and kind, and Nia felt like she might explode from the inside out. She remembered what her friends had told her about sex—how it was overrated—but Nia's experience was nothing like that. She knew the sex was special because her relationship with Cory was special. Turns out, her mom was right.

***

"Oh my God, I'm late," Nia said, frantically pulling up her period app. Sure enough, there it was, last week: *Period to start on May 9.* She looked at the calendar. It was May 23. With all the preparation for graduation she hadn't even realized she was two weeks late until she went under her bathroom counter to grab more toilet paper and saw her practically empty tampon box. *When was the last time I had my period*, she wondered.

She took a deep breath and drummed her fingers on the counter. Since that night in the cabin, she was almost embarrassed to say how many times she had had sex with Cory. They had unlocked the cap off their chemistry, and it was incredible every single time.

But now this. She was right on the cusp of being a full-fledged doctor, and there's no way a baby fit into her plans. They had used a condom every time, but Nia still felt uneasy.

She typed out a quick message to Cory. *I think I'm late.*

She wasn't happy to see the one-word answer he responded with: *Really?*

Yes, really.

A few seconds later her phone rang. "Babe, are you sure?"

"Yes, I'm sure. My period is usually pretty consistent and I'm two weeks late."

"Two weeks?" he said, his voice rising a bit.

"Yes, two weeks."

He paused for a moment. "Okay, so we'll go to the doctor and get a pregnancy test."

"Can you bring a pregnancy test over here?"

"You want to do one at home?"

"Yes. Because if I get a negative now it'll be a relief. I don't want to wait days to figure this out."

"Okay. I'll swing by and get one. Gimme about twenty minutes."

A half-hour later, Cory came in with a CVS bag and a bottle of ginger ale. "In case, you know," he said. "Trying to be thoughtful."

She grabbed the test and took it. "Come on in," she called from the bathroom. She sat on the bathroom floor, trying not to look at the stick on the counter.

Cory kneeled down with her. "What are you thinking?"

"I'm thinking that this can't be happening to me."

"Well, I'm not going anywhere. So we can get through this together."

"I appreciate that, Cory, really I do, but you don't know how this is going to work.

You will be able to start your residency like you planned, while I will have to stop and have this baby and have my whole career interrupted. Which isn't fair, because I worked just as hard as you to get here."

"I understand that," he said patiently. "But I'm here for you. And we can work this out so you can still be the doctor you want to be."

"I want to believe you," she said. She closed her eyes and put her head back against the cold tile. "I think it's been three minutes. Can you check?"

Cory picked up the stick and squinted. "What am I supposed to be looking for?"

"Two lines means I'm pregnant."

He paused. "I definitely see one line."

"Really?"

"Yes, really."

She scrambled up to look at the test herself. "One line. I'm not pregnant? So why am I so late?"

"You're probably just stressed with everything you've got going on. It's been a busy month, with an even more stressful month coming up."

"You're right." She took a deep breath. "I'm sorry I was so negative when you were just trying to be helpful."

"No, you were right," he said, sitting down next to her. "When we do decide to have kids, it will affect your career more than it will affect mine. But I want you to know that I love you and I think you will be a brilliant doctor. The world needs to see that. So I'll do whatever I can to make sure you get to be the doctor you want to be."

She held his face in her hands and kissed him. "I do love you."

"I know. Now let's go get some pizza to celebrate this 'I'm not pregnant' news." He picked her up off the floor and tossed her over his shoulder.

"Cory, put me down!" she yelled, pounding his shoulders and laughing.

"Not 'til we get some pizza in you. How about pepperoni?"

***

Nia tried to hold still as the makeup artist applied the mascara to her top lashes. She could not believe she was getting married in less than an hour. She had spent the previous three months planning and prepping for this moment, and now it was finally here. They had opted for a small ceremony, with only twenty or so of their closest friends and family at the Payne-Corley House. All of her besties from school would be there, except for April, who was out of the country. She sent a lovely gift though.

Cory had worked hard to get them three consecutive days off so they could travel to Atlanta for the wedding, as Nia had wanted. She hadn't seen Cory all day so she was really excited to see his face at the ceremony.

She was so certain that this was what she wanted.

Short pregnancy scare aside, their entire relationship had been so drama-free. There was no shouting, no fighting, none of the theatrics that some of her friends had dealt with. There were no crazed baby mamas, no lying, no cheating. Just a man who did what he said he would do when he said he would do it. Nia let out a low breath, thanking her lucky stars that she was able to meet and marry this guy who was crazy about her.

"You look so calm," Toya, the makeup artist, remarked.

"Really?" Nia replied, trying to only move her mouth and not any other part of her face.

"Yes, really. I do brides' makeup all the time and I usually have to keep some of those blotting sheets on me because they're sweating up a storm." Toya pulled out a slim black compact and went to work on Nia's eyelids.

"That's because she listened to her best friend," Patrice chimed in from the corner.

She adjusted her gold bridesmaid dress and came over to give the bride-to-be the once over. "You look *good*, girl. Cory is gonna cry when he sees you."

"Cory is not the type of guy who cries when he's happy," Nia said, smiling and rolling her eyes at her friend.

"Not on an ordinary day, but today, girl, I predict some tears!"

Felicia flew into the room, teetering on her four-inch heels that she insisted on wearing because according to her, "I never get to dress up anymore! I'm always in scrubs!"

"Are we ready yet?" she said, crossing the room, to sit next to Patrice. "Everyone out there is waiting."

"Everyone who?" Patrice said, laughing. "There's only like ten people."

"You know what I mean," Felicia said, poking her in the ribs. "I'm ready to get this party started. I saw Cory out there, looking handsome as ever."

"Alright then; you just about done, Toya?" Nia gestured for the mirror and checked out her friend's handiwork. "Beautiful!"

"You are so welcome," Toya said with a smile. She carefully bent down to give Nia a hug. "I didn't have to do much. You already look gorgeous. I just added color."

She pulled the white sheet off Nia that was protecting her wedding dress. They had opted for a small, nontraditional wedding and Nia went with a more nontraditional dress, a knee-length fitted white dress that she capped off with royal blue heels. Her mother had a fit and wanted her to pick something longer and more princess-like, but Nia insisted that she didn't want to spend hundreds of dollars on a dress she'd only wear once. This dress fit her personality, and she felt great in it. She'd shown Cory a picture of it and his reaction told her everything she needed to know: this was the dress.

She steadied herself and smiled at her two bridesmaids. "Y'all ready?"

"Ready," they said in unison. Toya kissed Nia on the cheek and wished her luck before slipping out the door.

Nia picked up her bouquet of flowers off the side table and nodded toward the door. "Okay, I'm ready." Patrice and Felicia opened the door and took their places at the front of the venue, next to the pastor. Cory and his best friends Shelton and Mike stood there proudly, chests puffed out, hands clasped in front of them. Cory wore the same black suit he wore to their engagement party, giving Nia a feeling of love and excitement as soon as they locked eyes.

Nia held out her arm for her father to link with her and, together, they made their way down the short aisle. Patrice was right—there was definitely a tear in Cory's eyes.

As they reached the end of the aisle and her father kissed her cheek to give her away, she reached out for Cory's hand and gripped it.

"The couple today has written their own vows," the pastor said to the audience assembled. He nodded to Nia for her to go first.

Nia unfolded the piece of paper that was tucked into her bouquet and began to read.

"Cory, I have been in love with you for four years and every day you show me you love me. You are my rock, my refuge, my best friend, and I am so fortunate to be beginning this life with you. Thank you for loving me the way that you do."

The pastor smiled and nodded to Cory. "Your turn, young man."

Cory stood up straight and cleared his throat. "I tried to write down my vows but I had the hardest time, so I figured I would just freestyle it."

Their friends and family laughed, but Cory got serious. He held her hands in his and looked directly into her eyes. "My friends asked me yesterday if I was nervous about getting married, especially since we haven't been engaged that long. But I told them that I was more sure about this than anything in my life.

I am so happy that you are going to be my wife because there is no one else I see myself with. We just work, Nia. And I can't wait to see what the future holds for us. I love you."

He stepped forward to kiss her but the pastor interjected. "Uh-uh, not yet."

Everyone laughed and Cory winked. "We gotta hurry up and get to that part!"

"By the power vested in me, I now pronounce you husband and wife. Now, you may kiss your bride."

Cory placed both hands on the side of her face and kissed her. Everyone clapped and cheered and Nia smiled so hard she knew her cheeks would hurt the next day.

The newlyweds retreated to the private room off to the side for a few quiet moments while their wedding party headed next door to get ready for the reception. Cory touched his forehead to his wife's.

"How are you doing?" he asked.

"We're married," she said, smiling. "That's how I'm doing."

"I'm thinking we should do this every year," he said, leaning back on the side table. "You get all cute in your dress, I throw on a suit and we have a party. You down?"

"You gonna spend this money every year?" she joked.

"We're gonna be rich, baby! You're looking at a future anesthesiologist married to an OB/GYN. I give the epidurals and you catch the babies. We're a perfect team."

A knock on the door interrupted their conversation. Felicia poked her head in. "We're ready for you."

Cory held out his hand and Nia took it. "We're coming."

They walked out together, ready to enjoy the rest of their wedding.

Let's Talk

Have you ever thought about if you want to get married? It's a big step, and one that involves a certain level of maturity if you want to make it last.

So much of our culture shows the worst of marriage —you see celebrities getting married and divorced in the same time it takes you to scroll through your Twitter feed, people having babies without any thought of a wedding (or at the very least engagement) and more.

Getting married might not even seem like the cool thing to do any more.

I've looked at recent research, and the trend is clear --people are getting married less frequently now than they did in the past. In addition, there's a trend toward cohabitation, where couples just live together instead of getting married.

I think every couple has to figure out what works best for them, but that starts with *you* figuring out what's best for you.

My goal is for every young woman I interact with to be confident in what she wants in life and in love and to know how to get it. If you want to get married, but a guy only wants to live with you, I want you to be confident in telling him how you feel. If a guy wants to marry you, but you're not ready (or don't think he's the one), I want you to be confident in telling him you'd like to wait.

I love the love story that Nia and Cory have. Nia kissed a few frogs in her life, but with Cory, she's found someone who loves her and isn't afraid to show it. What I love most of all is how compatible they are. They are both smart, funny, ambitious and kind. They fit well together. While Cory is cute, he also makes a good partner because he's kind. He pays attention to Nia and looks for ways to surprise her and delight her.

Nia wasn't afraid to be alone. She didn't want to settle for a random, not-quite-right guy just to say she was in a relationship. She waited for someone who matched her, someone who made her feel safe.

Do you feel safe? That's the main question I want you to ask yourself when you are dating. And not just physical safety, but mental and emotional safety as well. Do you feel comfortable talking about your feelings with him? Are you usually in a better or worse mood after you talk to him? Does he add to your life or does he drain you?

Of course, even the most amazing relationship is not without conflict. Whenever you have a dilemma in your relationship, talk about it. Get it out in the open. Communication is the only way through. If you're wrong, apologize. It makes your relationship stronger and helps you grow as an individual.

On the journal pages that follow, I want you to think about what a healthy and loving relationship looks like to you. What kind of partner do you want to attract? Yes, it's important to be happy and whole on your own, but if you do want someone to date and hang out with, think about how that person fits into your life. Do they add to your happiness or subtract from it?

What You Should Know — Healthy Relationships

Research has shown that one of the biggest life decisions you can make is who you marry. A supportive partner will allow you to pursue your career with more focus and determination because they are not threatened by your success, and they want you to succeed as much you do. Do you know what you want your future relationships to look like? Take a moment to finish these journal prompts on healthy relationships.

A healthy relationship is:

I want a partner who is:

I want to be a partner who is:

Chapter Twelve: 2 as 1

"I can't believe you have me out here," Nia huffed as she worked her way up the hill. "You know I hate cold weather."

"This was your idea," Cory said, beads of sweat popping up on his forehead despite the chill. "You're the one who said we had to find a time to work out together."

"Yeah, but I meant inside. Not when it's 30 degrees and slushy outside." As soon as she said it, she slipped on a patch of ice and grabbed Cory's arm for support.

"Let's get inside before you bust your head wide open," he said, laughing.

They scurried back to the hospital, stomping off their feet as they made their way back down the hall. "Are you on-call tonight?" Cory asked, checking his calendar on his phone.

"No, I'm off tonight, thankfully," she said. "You're on-call, though, right?"

"Right."

She frowned. "I know I was happy when we got matched together, but our schedules are always completely opposite. I feel like I haven't seen you all week."

"You saw me today," Cory said optimistically with a weak shrug.

"For like ten minutes," she said, pouting.

She hadn't anticipated how difficult it would be to complete her residency and be a newlywed. Some of her professors had advised against getting married until after they had completed their residencies, but Nia didn't understand why she would wait four years before marrying the love of her life when he was already right in front of her.

Now she kind of realized they had a point. It was really hard to spend any quality time together when they were both swamped with patients and paperwork. As first-year residents at the hospital, they were the low man on the totem pole and got stuck with all the extra work that the attending physicians didn't want to do.

Nia had just spent forty-eight hours on call, sleeping in spurts in the on-call room on the fourth floor of the hospital. Oddly enough, she enjoyed these stretches because she felt like she was thrown into all kinds of situations that she had to figure out on the fly. She liked working with women in their various stages of life – early adolescence, pregnancy and menopause. She had been a great medical student, but now she had to put all the knowledge to use on real patients who looked to her as a capable doctor.

The deliveries were her favorite. She had delivered one hundred babies so far in the first two months of residency, and each one was a completely different experience. She finally got to deliver twins, which was probably the highlight of her residency so far. The first time she had delivered a baby, back in medical school, she was in awe of the power of women and how something so primal and natural could also be so beautiful. Now she'd had enough experience that she wasn't mentally running through the steps of delivery. She was able to just connect with the mom and help her dig deep to push the baby out. Two weeks ago, a mom was so impressed with her work that she gave her baby the middle name Nia.

Cory had started his anesthesiology residency and spent most of his time away from the hospital with his nose in his textbooks. Nia tried not to bother him when he was studying. Now that she lived with him, she got a good idea of how he liked to spend his time when he wasn't with her. He was a homebody, usually exhausted from working long shifts, so most of their date nights (what few they had) were spent on the couch with Chinese takeout and Netflix. She noticed it didn't take long for that habit to show up on their waistlines, so she asked Cory to start working out with her.

She had been naturally slim her whole life so working out every day was weird for her, and she didn't like it.

Cory humored her and still adored her though. Because their schedules were so wacky, they weren't able to see each other much during the day. Cory made a point of keeping an ongoing text conversation throughout the workday. It brightened her mood whenever a message from him came through.

In the hallway, Cory grabbed her hand, breaking through her thoughts. "Hey, here's what we'll do," he said. "We haven't been out anywhere in a while so let's take some time tomorrow, when we're both off, and go on a real date."

Nia looked at him skeptically. "A real date? You sure you have the energy for that?"

"Of course," he said confidently. "Anything for my wife."

Hearing Cory call her "my wife" still gave Nia butterflies, so she took him at his word that he wouldn't fall asleep during their date. "Where are we going?" she asked.

"How about Valerio's?" he suggested, his eyes lighting up. Since it was the location of their first date and engagement party, the restaurant continued to hold romantic significance for the two of them.

"Okay, that sounds good," she said. She hugged him quickly and checked the time on her phone.

"Don't you need to get going?"

"I do. What do you have planned for your day off?"

"Sleep," Nia said quickly. "Just like…hours of sleep. I'm exhausted."

"Be sure you rest up then." He kissed her on the forehead. "I'll see you tomorrow."

***

"They changed the menu," Nia said, looking over the selections in front of her. "They don't have my favorite pasta dish anymore."

"The lemon one?"

"Yeah," she said. "Oh well."

"We've been coming here for a while," Cory joked with her. "We're getting old. They're switching up the menu on us!"

Nia looked over the menu to try to find something else to eat when the waitress appeared with her notepad ready to take their order.

"Are you two ready or do you need a moment?" she asked, clicking her pen.

"Actually, I have a question," Cory said. "I brought my wife here for a special date. We actually had our first date here. She loves that one lemon and artichoke pasta dish that you used to have but we don't see it on the menu anymore. Is there anyway the chef could, I dunno, make it with the ingredients he has in the back?"

"Cory, it's okay—" Nia interjected.

The waitress smiled. "Well, let me see what I can do."

She turned back to the kitchen. Nia looked at her husband in awe. "Oh, you didn't have to do that. I could have just ordered something else."

He shrugged. "You don't know if you don't ask, right?"

A few minutes later the waitress reappeared. "You're in luck. The dish you like is on our specials menu, and it's on the menu for tomorrow night, which means we have the ingredients in the back. Our chef remembered you had your engagement party here and is happy to treat such important guests. We can get that right out for you."

Nia was stunned. "Wow. Thank you."

Cory smiled at his wife. "See. Perfect. Thank you so much."

The waitress took Cory's order and headed back to the kitchen to put it in. The newlyweds sat and sipped wine slowly, not wanting to rush through the evening ahead. They both knew nights like this wouldn't come along that often.

"Do you ever think maybe we should have waited to get married?" Nia asked.

"No."

"Just no? You don't want to elaborate?"

"No." He smiled.

"But come on. I can't be the only one who thinks this is harder than I imagined. We are working seventy hours a week, on opposite schedules, trying to save money so we can eventually pay off these student loans."

"And how would not being married help that?" He took a sip of his wine.

"I don't know. I just want to focus on work, but I also want to focus on being married. There's not enough time to focus on everything."

"You want to know my secret?" he said, leaning in toward Nia. "I don't worry."

"That doesn't help me!" Nia said, laughing.

"Why not?"

"Because. Worrying comes naturally to me."

"What are you worried about? Let's get it out on the table."

Nia took a deep breath. "I think we're too busy these days. I always imagined when I got married that I would, I dunno, actually see my husband every day."

"But you do see me. Most of the time."

"You know what I mean."

He nodded. "Well, do you want me to quit? I can go get a job at Home Depot," he joked. "Get you a discount on your gardening tools."

"You play too much."

Cory took this moment to get serious. "I know what you're talking about. I thought that since we managed pretty well during med school that we could handle residency with no problem. But it's different. I have to do so much reading to keep up and make my name known in the operating room. And I don't want you to feel like I'm neglecting you."

"I don't think you're neglecting me. I know you're doing your best. I'm just missing you, that's all. As long as we are able to talk and hang out together, it'll be fine."

"Good."

Just then their dishes came out and Nia's lemon pasta dish was every bit of amazing as she had remembered. "Thank you for asking them to make this," she said, wiping sauce from her bottom lip. "It's so good."

"You're welcome," he said, winking.

Nia looked around at the restaurant, filled with other couples who were on dates. She noticed they weren't really talking to each other, instead scrolling through their phones or just eating in silence. Nia shuddered and hoped that wasn't what they were going to look like in a few years.

"What do you think about moving to Atlanta after our residencies are over?"

Cory took a sip of water. "I didn't realize you wanted to do that."

Nia took a deep breath. "I enjoy Cleveland. I do. And I like that your parents are here.

But it hasn't really felt like home to me. Not in the way Atlanta does."

Cory just nodded and let her continue. "I was thinking back to our pregnancy scare last year. You remember?"

"How could I forget?" He laughed.

"Do you ever think about having kids?"

"Sure. Not for a while, but yeah, I've thought about it."

"When do you think would be a good time?"

"Probably not for a while," he said, scratching his head. "When would we even have time to make a baby?"

She swatted his arm and laughed. "Well, I was thinking that when we do have kids, I wouldn't mind raising them in Atlanta. It's warmer, there's a ton of job opportunities and my parents are there, so they could help raise them."

"Well, my parents are here," he pointed out. "So they could help us if we had a kid here."

"Yes, but your parents work more than we do," she said. "What's your mom going to do, bring our baby into her clinic?"

Cory let out a deep sigh. "You're right."

"It's not something we have to decide right now," she said. "Just a conversation."

"But it's something we should discuss," he agreed. "I hadn't thought about moving to Atlanta but it would make sense."

"We still have a while to think about it," she said, stuffing more of the delicious pasta into her mouth. "We'll be here for at least a few more years. I'm a planner. You know how I am."

"Yes, I do," he said. "And that's why I love you." He leaned across the table to kiss her and she blushed.

"You ready for some dessert?" she asked.

"Always."

They got a piece of cheesecake to go and walked out of the restaurant, feeling great about where they were in their relationship. When they got home, Nia kicked off her shoes and plopped down on the couch, ready to dig into the cheesecake.

"Save me some," Cory called as he shrugged out of his coat. He hadn't even made his way over to the couch before his pager went off. "Bad news, babe. I've got to go up to the hospital."

"Again?" she said, putting down the fork.

"Yup. But hopefully it won't be too long."

"I'll wait up?"

"No, it's okay. Just go on to sleep. I know you're exhausted." He kissed her on her forehead and slipped his coat back on. "Text you when I'm done."

"I love you, Cory."

"I love you too."

Chapter Thirteen: 3 is a Happy Family

Five Years Later

"Cory, hurry up!"

Nia clapped her hands and reached out for Imani, their 10-month-old daughter, who had just pushed herself up on her chubby legs into a standing position. "She's about to take her first steps, Cory! Hurry!"

Cory flew into the living room from the kitchen. "Did I miss it?"

"No. Looks like she's still thinking about it."

Imani stood in the middle of the living room, looking over at her dad and grinning, drool dripping down her face. Cory bent over and reached his hands out to her. "Come here, baby girl! Come to daddy!"

She wiggled in place and took one unsteady stride forward. Nia clapped and cheered.

"Who knew that something as small as walking could be so exciting?" she said to Cory.

Imani took one more wobbly step and fell, her diaper cushioning her fall. Cory scooped her up and kissed her on the cheek.

"You know, I think she's starting to look more like me," Cory joked.

"Boy, you know good and well she is my twin. From the hair to the nose to the lips. She is all me."

"She's got my chin!" Cory said, putting his face next to Imani's.

"Your chin? That's all you can claim, huh?"

"You're the one who turned your body into a cloning lab."

"Hey, the least she could do is come out looking like me after all I went through to have her." As excited as Nia was to be pregnant, the pregnancy was hard, with morning sickness and random aches and pains the whole way through. She was constantly tired and wondered how on earth she managed to create a little human and see patients all at the same time.

It helped that they had relocated to Atlanta, where Nia's parents were over all the time, trying to gobble up their first granddaughter. Even PJ, who had just graduated from Clark Atlanta, did his fair share of babysitting. As much as they could, Cory's parents came down to see Imani, delighting in being first-time grandparents.

Things had calmed down a bit, with Cory taking a position at Emory and Nia joining a private practice in midtown Atlanta. She was able to have better control over her schedule, which came in handy now that she was a mom.

"I've got to get ready to go," Nia said, gesturing for Cory to hand Imani over so she could give her a goodbye hug and kiss. "The girls are expecting me." Nia hated leaving Imani, but she also enjoyed doing her community work.

Cory glanced at the clock. "I didn't realize you were speaking today."

"Every third Saturday of the month," she reminded him in a sing-song voice. She nuzzled her daughter's cheeks and begrudgingly handed her back to her dad. She'd be back soon enough to get in more cuddles.

***

"Ladies, can you give a round of applause to Dr. Nia Patterson?"

The thirty-or-so young ladies assembled in the community center meeting room clapped politely for Nia as she made her way to the front.

GIRLS on a Mission was one of her favorite community organizations and Nia loved coming in to speak with the girls every month. They were all teenagers, with the exception of a few mentor girls who were in their early twenties.

They all had questions: *What do you do when a boy likes you? Can you really get pregnant the first time you have sex? What if your boyfriend wants to have sex and you don't? What if you want to have sex but are scared to talk to your parents about it?*

She remembered what it was like being a young girl just full of curiosity, and she considered these talks her way of paying it forward.

"Okay, ladies, you know the drill. Queens ready?" she asked, calling them to attention. "Queens ready? Crown on!" was their favorite call and response to begin the meeting.

"Crown on!" they called out in unison.

"I don't think I heard you. Queens ready?"

"Crown on!"

"Perfect." Nia sat down in the middle of the circle. "Where did we leave off last month?"

Katrina, a bright 16-year-old with purple streaks in her hair, raised her hand. "We were talking about you in college, how you went to Spelman."

"That's right, yes. Most of you are getting ready to go to college, correct?"

They all nodded their heads and looked around at their peers.

"And so what questions do you have for me?"

The conversation flowed easily from one topic to the other and by the time the hour was up, Nia was pleased with the connection she'd made with the girls. As she was leaving, Katrina came up to her with a final question.

"Is it okay if I text you sometime?" she asked. "I can't really talk to my mom about some of this stuff."

"Of course," Nia said. She exchanged numbers with Katrina. "Let's work on figuring out ways that we can get your mom in the loop, though, okay?"

Katrina nodded, gave Nia a hug and went back to the group.

As Nia put her phone back in her pocket, she felt a random piece of paper and pulled it out, thinking it was an old receipt. It was a note from Cory. *I am so proud of you. Every day you amaze me more. Love you, C.*

Nia smiled to herself. She couldn't wait to get home.

Sources

- Grimes, J. (2008). Seductive Delusions: How Everyday People Catch STIs. Baltimore: Johns Hopkins University Press.
- Logan Levkoff, J. W. (2014). Got Teens? The Doctor Moms' Guide to Sexuality, Social Media and Other Adolescent Realities. Berkeley: Seal Press.
- Oz, M. F. (2011). You, The Owner's Manual for Teens: A Guide to a Healthy Body and Happy Life. New York: Scribner.
- https://www.aids.gov/hiv-aids-basics/hiv-aids-101/what-is-hiv-aids/
- https://health.clevelandclinic.org/2015/02/tired-of-tampons-here-are-pros-and-cons-of-menstrual-cups/
- http://www.cdc.gov/nchs/fastats/marriage-divorce.htm
- https://bedsider.org/
- http:www.advocatesforyouth.org/publications/publications-a-z/413-adolescent-sexual-behavior-i-demographics
- https://www.guttmacher.org/fact-sheet/american-teens-sexual-and-reproductive-health
- www.cdc.gov/hepatitis/

NIA & THE NUMBERS GAME, *A Teenager's Guide to Education, Relationships & Sex by Dr. Kela Henry*

Please visit www.DrKelaHenry.com for special offers, contests, give-a ways and important resources for a college education.

Let me know what you think about NIA & THE NUMBERS GAME. Looking forward to hearing from you! You can e-mail me directly at: drkelahenry@gmail.com

For speaking requests, book signings, permission to print or use excerpts from this book please contact: info@keymediapublicrelations.com

Books Make Great Gifts! *NIA & THE NUMBERS GAME, A Teenager's Guide to Education, Relationships & Sex is a great gift for teenagers, parents, grandparents' — everyone can relate to NIA!*

Published by BTH Creations LLC